KEEPING TIME

Colby Rodowsky

FARRAR STRAUS GIROUX

New York

Copyright © 1983 Colby Rodowsky
All rights reserved
Library of Congress catalog card number: 83-14122
Published simultaneously in Canada
by Collins Publishers, Toronto
Printed in the United States of America
Designed by Stephen Roxburgh
First edition, 1983

In memory of my mother and father

KEEPING TIME

1

IT WAS THE PART of town where the streets were narrow and paved with cobblestones. The part of town that had grown there on the side of the river when the city was just beginning, falling into a pattern of streets and alleyways. In time it had become a jumble of warehouses and wharves and small thin houses that were new, then old, then new again as people moved away from them and then others moved back down to the water's edge.

Drew Wakeman stood at the end of Fell Street and heard himself speaking in his father's voice.

He heard Gunther's words tumbling out of his own mouth, gruff in the way that Gunther was sometimes gruff. "I told you guys—we've got a show tonight. At the harbor. Besides, you don't know what it's like. The competition out on the streets."

"You've always got a show," said Jake.

"Anyway, it's the Orioles we're talking about, man. Not sandlot, or Little League. The O-ri-oles," said Hank.

"A twi-night double header. Against the Yankees. And we're going to go—take the bus uptown—sit in the bleachers, and eat popcorn," said Tom.

"Come on."

"Yeah, just this once."

"Tell your father you want a night off."

"You crazy or something?" said Drew. "A summer night, and I'm going to tell my father I want it off? He'd skin me alive. Tar and feather me."

"How about in winter?" said Hank. "You go to school. You stay home at night and do homework and all."

"But in winter we don't perform as much," said Drew. "Sometimes just on weekends, if the weather's good. That's how come in winter Gunther and Nicholas and Kate have to wait tables and be dishwashers and stuff like that. So we can be free to go back onto the streets in spring. Because we *have* to go back."

"It's child abuse," said Jake.

"Worse than the sweatshops," said Hank.

"Why can't you deliver papers or groceries, or sweep sidewalks like the rest of us do," said Tom. "Anyway, I'll bet you never even asked if you could miss a show."

For a minute Drew stood still, watching his three friends as they moved onto the wooden pier that jutted out from the end of the street into the water. A tugboat plied its way up the channel and Drew waited until it disappeared behind a rusted shed before he followed them, lapsing back into his Gunther words. "It's all part of a tradition, reaching back to minstrels and jongleurs and troubadours and waits."

"Criminy, you sound like they were your ancestors or something," said Jake.

"They were, sort of," said Drew.

"But you're just street performers," said Hank.

"Yeah, but so were they, in a way. We're buskers," said Drew.

"Son of a busker," whooped Jake.

"Son of a busker," called the other two, their voices soaring and mingling with the cries of the gulls that swooped and darted at the river.

"Old S.O.B. Wakeman," said Jake.

"S.O.B. Wakeman . . ."

"S.O.B. . . ."

And the boys danced and jiggled, pushing at each other, slapping the sides of their legs, swinging around to clap Drew on the back, until finally they collapsed in a heap, laughing and rocking sideways. Then they lay back, feeling the warmth of the boards beneath them, the late-afternoon sun beating down.

"We got to go," said Hank, pulling himself up. "Come on, Drew, it's your last chance."

"Don't be a chump," said Jake. "You could say you have a sore throat."

"Say your voice is changing. Say anything, so long as you don't wimp out on us."

For a minute Drew wanted to go to the ball game more than he ever remembered wanting anything before. He closed his eyes and heard the thwack of ball against bat, the cheering of the crowd. He saw the players running out of the dugout, and the umpires in their dark blue suits. He felt the grit of the bleachers and smelled the roasting peanuts. But even then he heard himself going on. "Gunther says, before my voice changes, they might as well take advantage of it while they can."

The three boys started to edge away.

"Besides," Drew called, raising his voice as if trying to draw them back. "There's this new song—new to me, I mean—that we're doing tonight. *Greensleeves* it's called, and at practice I kept messing it up. And anyway"—his voice boomed out as if it were coming from somebody else—"I like to sing, so what do you think of that?"

Tom waited until the other two had moved away before he leaned toward Drew and said, "I like it, too. The music you all play. I like the rhythm, and the songs, and the way everybody closes in around you guys. Even the way they leave money is okay. But yikes, I like baseball, too."

Hank came back toward them. "Hey, man," he said, pointing his finger at Drew. "It's up to you, but Baltimore here's a Major League town. And the Orioles are a Major League team. To be Major League, you got to act Major League. You don't belong here. Man, you might as well be in East Podunk or Ashtabula or Newark, New Jersey."

The boys turned, walking at first, then breaking into a run.

"Sing pretty, Mr. Greensleeves," called Jake.

". . . Mr. Greentrees . . ."

". . . Mr. Greencheese . . ."

"Sing pretty, tweety bird."

I do belong here, thought Drew as he watched them go. I do—I do—I do. He balanced himself along the railroad tracks that ran down the middle of the street, and knew that this was the way he had felt ever since the day six years ago when he climbed out of the van that brought them all from California and Gunther said, "Enough. We're not going any farther."

Drew stood for a minute looking toward his friends who had gone. He kicked a Coke can and heard it clatter as it bounced along the cobblestones. Then he turned, flopping onto the flat white wooden step in front of his house.

"Losers," he muttered under his breath. "Dumb old stupid losers." He clamped his teeth on his lower lip, his thoughts racing on. Anyway—who cares? I don't even like baseball. I didn't even want to go.

Drew slammed his foot on a large black ant inching its way along the brick sidewalk. He pulled his foot back quickly, hoping the ant had escaped.

There was only a slight smudge on the brick.

Clang, a sound came from inside the house. *Clang*, it came again.

Drew squinted up at the screen door, trying to see through the picture painted there of trees and swans and a wandering blue lake. He could just make out the shape of his father as he swung two large pot lids together as if they were cymbals. "It's time," Gunther called against the reverberations that filled the air. "We should move out early. There's a lot going on tonight, not just at the harbor, but all around."

Drew pressed his face against the screen so he could see Gunther pacing around the small room delivering his message up the stairway and through the open kitchen door: "There's some kind of celebration tonight—a block party—and I thought we'd try for a spot along Cheapside Street. They're blocking off the street at both ends. Let's get an early start."

Drew opened the door and went inside, through the living room and the dining room, where Gunther was once again hunched over his crossword puzzle. He went down one step, through the long and narrow kitchen, and out the back door to the yard, which was also long, and a scant twelve feet wide—the width of the house.

Nicholas was juggling rings. Six of them, all different colors. He moved quickly, darting from side to side, slipping and sliding. His red tights, his white tunic, and his shoulder-length silver hair blended and spun themselves out, until he slowed and sank onto one knee and caught the rings one at a time, around his neck.

Drew waited until the last ring was caught before he moved forward, saying, "Hey, neat. You going to do that tonight?"

"I might indeed, sir. And then again I might not," said Nicholas, getting up and scooping a sweater off the fence and arranging it over his shoulders. "Got to keep the shoulders from tightening up. Won't be doing much of anything if the shoulders tighten up on me."

"Yeah, well, it's time to get ready, only nobody's moving yet."

"That's just fine, sir. Means we'll have a head start on the kitchen. First pickings at the fridge. Come on, let's go." And Nicholas dropped one arm around Drew's shoulders and moved him in the direction of the kitchen, the many-colored rings still bobbing around his neck.

A large orange cat jumped down from the fence and led the way, walking sturdily like a dog, and not slinking gracefully the way the other cats Drew saw did. She jumped up onto the counter, sliding on a stack of newspapers and sending an empty cornflakes box onto the floor.

"That cat, sir, is a klutz," said Nicholas, flexing his shoulder muscles and poking at the collection of dirty dishes in the sink. "I meant to get at this kitchen today," he said, washing a yellow mixing bowl and shaking it to get the water off.

"If you had, then everybody else would have decided to clean the kitchen, too. That's the way around here. Either everybody cleans or nobody does. Everybody goes to market or nobody goes. All without telling anyone." Drew opened a can of tuna fish and put a few chunks in the cat's saucer, then dumped the rest into an empty cereal bowl. He rooted in the refrigerator and pulled out a wilted stalk of celery and a jar of mayonnaise.

"That's called feast or famine, sir," said Nicholas, cracking eggs into a bowl. "Feast or famine."

"Is somebody making an omelette?" asked Gunther from the kitchen door. "If there's enough, I might have some—but if there's not, I'll just have cheese."

Without saying anything, Nicholas took three more eggs out of the refrigerator and did a quick juggling routine before cracking them.

"Now, don't anybody say a word," said Kate, rushing into the kitchen holding up a paint roller coated with white. "I know I'm not ready yet, but I will be. I just wanted to get the gesso on the wall, so the smell would fade before tonight. I'll grab some fruit and . . ." Her voice drifted off as she put her head into the refrigerator.

"You gessoed the wall again?" asked Betina from the doorway.

"Not the harbor scene," said Drew. "I liked it best." He peered at the roller that Kate still clutched in her hand, as if he somehow expected to see ships at dock tangled around its white nubby surface. "Why did you, huh?"

"Oh, I don't know," said Kate, pulling back out of the refrigerator. "Nothing lasts forever, and what I think I want there now is an object—one single object. An acorn, or maybe a shell."

"But, Kate," said Drew.

"No hassling," said Gunther, polishing an apple on the seat of his jeans and tossing it to Kate. "It's up to her."

"But an acorn, for Pete's sake," said Drew, as he squeezed past Betina and headed for the kitchen door. He ducked as his sister reached for half his sandwich, and said over his shoulder, "There's more in the bowl, or at least there was a minute ago."

"None for me," said Kate. "An apple is enough for now, and maybe later I'll get . . ."

"Here's an extra bagel half if anybody . . ."

"A plate for the omelette, if you please, sir . . ."

"I think the cat ate the rest of the tuna fish. Somebody hand me a can of soup . . ."

Drew balanced his plate on top of his glass of milk and edged his way out the door. He took a deep breath, glad to be away from the cluttered little kitchen. At the end of the yard he straddled a bench, putting his plate and glass down in front of him, and slowly began to eat.

From inside came the sound of voices and running water, the closing of cupboard doors and the scraping of chairs across the floor. Drew finished his sandwich and drank the rest of his milk. He watched them all—Poppa,

Kate, Betina, and Nicholas—as they appeared in the open kitchen door, moving back and forth.

There was Gunther, his father—the musician and leader of the group—who, to Drew, always seemed to be crowded around with his guitars and banjos. And there was Kate, who sang and played the dulcimer and the mandolin, who painted detailed scenes all over the walls of the house. Kate wasn't Drew's real mother, or his stepmother either, but she had been around so long she might as well have been.

There was Betina, his sister, who used to tell him Winnie-the-Pooh stories every night at bedtime and taught him to use chopsticks and to tie his shoelaces. After Betina came Nicholas, the juggler, who wasn't related to them at all, or to anyone else, as far as Drew could tell.

Sometimes when Drew thought about his family he liked to think about his real mother, too. Betina, who was five years older than he and remembered these things, told him that before Beth got leukemia and died, she and Gunther used to take the two children out onto the streets with them when they sang. Sometimes Drew pretended to himself that he remembered his mother swaying him back and forth in a canvas sling, in time with the music. He didn't really, any more than he could recall the times back in San Francisco when Nicholas and Kate had lived in the same rooming house with them, or how when Beth got sick they had helped take care of her, and of him and Betina.

Stretching out flat on the bench, Drew locked his hands behind his head and looked up at the sky.

"Hey, move over," said Betina, sitting on the end of the bench and pushing at his feet. "Here. I hid these two brownies yesterday and—a miracle—they were still there. What're you thinking?"

"Oh, just stuff. That I'm glad you did—hide the brownies," Drew said, sitting up and licking his lips.

"What else?"

"That I wish she wouldn't." ˎ

"Who wouldn't what?"

"Kate. Whiten out the harbor scene."

"Yeah, but you know Poppa. 'Don't hassle.' 'Everybody does his own thing around here.' 'We don't infringe,' " Betina said in the same Gunther voice that Drew had used earlier. She got up and drifted around the yard, saying, "Well, Kate'd better paint fast is all I can say."

"Why fast?" said Drew.

"If she wants me to see it. I might not be here after a while. Not for an acorn or anything else."

"Yeah," said Drew, stretching out on the bench again. "I've heard that before."

"It's okay for you now, but wait'll you're older. Then it won't seem so okay—standing around on street corners singing and hoping nobody you know sees you. Never really wanting to bring anybody home because everything's always a hodgepodge here. And the way Poppa just sort of lets things *happen*. Anyway," said Betina, slipping into a singsong voice, "up until now I didn't have any place to go."

"And now you do?"

"And now I do."

"Where, Betina?" said Drew, propping himself up on one elbow.

"Hmmmm," she said, pulling a leaf off a mulberry tree.

"Where?" said Drew, sitting all the way up.

"That's for me to know and you to find out."

Drew swung around and faced the other way, his back to his sister. He was determined not to beg her the way Betina had always wanted him to when they were younger and she knew something he didn't. He counted backwards by threes from one hundred, and when he got to fifty-eight, he heard her turn and go back into the house, the screen door slamming shut behind her.

Then suddenly it was as though someone had dropped an ice cube down his back. What if Betina meant it this time? What if she really did have some place to go?

He tried to push away the cold slithery thought, wondering instead what picture Kate was going to paint next, trying to remember the words of the new song they were to sing that night.

He heard his father call. "Come on, Drew. It's time for you to bring the cart. Time to get this show on the road."

2

DREW WENT over the high fence as easily as if it had been a doorsill. He took a shortcut across the vacant lot, stepping around holes and over roots and cinder blocks. He scaled another wooden fence and dropped into the yard of the garage on the other side. Unchaining the cart, he dragged it through the gate, bumping it along the street to the front of the house.

The rest of them were poised there waiting. Then, as if by the flip of a switch, they went into action. Kate handed things through the door to Betina to Nicholas to Drew and finally to Gunther, who arranged them in the cart. A bucket brigade of campstools, blankets, banjos, guitars, a mandolin and a dulcimer, recorders, flutes, and a string bag of red rubber balls. From inside the mandolin case came a muffled twang as Nicholas's torches were wedged down next to it. Betina tossed a black silk top hat to Drew, who fit it into the cart just as Gunther pulled the tarp over it all.

Drew knelt down to tie his shoe, broke the lace, and had to knot it. His knee vibrated with the rumble of cart wheels against cobblestones, and for a minute he stayed where he was, watching the others as they started up the street. Gunther, in jeans and a shirt, his shoes worn thin, pushed the cart. Kate walked on one side of him, her layers of skirts and leotards wrapped all around with a red fringed shawl. Nicholas was on the other side, high-stepping and bowing to people on the streets, a hole in his tights showing his white shorts underneath.

Betina was a few paces behind them, a set of earphones on her head. She held the Walkman in her hand, and her body moved to the music that only she could hear.

Drew came at the end of the little procession: not too tall, and slight, his shaggy brown hair curling just below his ears. His jeans were faded white along the seams, and across the back of his blue T-shirt was a ship in full sail.

As Betina rounded the corner, Drew scrambled after her, calling, "Hey—wait. Be-tin-a." Catching up, he had to tug at her arm to get her attention.

"You look like something from outer space," he said when she turned to face him.

"Huh?" she said.

"Outer space," he called. "With the earphones and the dark glasses."

"Oh," said Betina, turning a knob on the Walkman. "I didn't hear you. What'd you say?"

"Just that you look like—never mind."

They walked along Thames Street, past the waterfront lined with tugs and police boats. Betina turned the volume up and snatches of music oozed out of the orange foam-rubber earpieces. The crowds on the sidewalk swirled around them, and Gunther and the others disappeared.

Drew nudged Betina, waiting until she turned the music down again before he said, "Come on. We don't want to lose them."

"What difference does it make? We know where they're going."

But still Drew craned his neck trying to keep the rest of them in sight. Waiting for a beer truck to pass, they turned off Broadway onto a side street where narrow brick houses had been restored.

"Hey, Betina," said Drew, half turning toward her. "Take off your earphones for a minute. There's something I want to—I mean—"

"They're okay. I can hear around them as long as the music's off," she said, her fingers hovering just above the ON/OFF switch.

"What I—well—how come you said what you did before?" said Drew, getting the words out all in a rush.

"What?"

"How now you have some place to go. How now you won't be here to see what Kate's going to paint next."

"How now, brown cow," said Betina, dancing out in front, then turning to face him. "How—now—brown—cow—"

"What did you *mean*?" he said.

Betina waited for him to catch up, without saying anything. A U-Haul lumbered by, and the two of them moved closer to the curb, then back out into the street after it had passed.

"Think about it for a minute," she said. "The way we

live. The way things are with us. Think about Poppa and how he took to the streets and never went back."

"I know about that," said Drew. "But things were different then—in the sixties."

"But didn't you ever really think about him doing that? And how Poppa must have had a mother and father, same as Beth must have had a mother and father. Didn't it ever occur to you, Andrew Wakeman, that someplace we might have grandparents?"

Drew looked up ahead, spotting Gunther and the others just as they were rounding the corner, Nicholas bowing to a woman in an upstairs window.

"Grandparents?" he said. "Yeah, well, no. I guess maybe because we've always had the others. Nicholas and Kate, I mean."

Betina laughed. "I don't think Kate'd much like being thought of as a grandmother type—she's way younger even than Poppa."

"It's just that she was there. Taking me to kindergarten and to the doctor that time I walked on a nail. And Nicholas taught me to play ball."

"I don't have anything *against* them," said Betina. "I know they helped out when Beth was sick. And after she died they both stayed on, because by then we had all just drifted into one another, and with this bunch, once we drift we stay drifted."

"Then we left California and came East. And you threw up the entire way and we kept stopping places till you stopped throwing up," said Drew. And as he talked he found himself remembering bits of that trip across the country in Gunther's van: town blending into town, and roads that never seemed to end, cold Coca-Colas and the smell of dusty heat. He remembered Betina with her head in Nicholas's lap, and the gentle sound of Kate and Gunther's singing.

"We were heading for New York," Betina said.

"Only you threw up once too often, and we got as far as Baltimore and stopped and never left."

"Except I'm going now," Betina said. "Because, whether you care or not, we might have grandparents out there who live ordinary kinds of lives, and I'm going to find them. Just you wait and see." Betina stopped talking, in a way that Drew knew meant she wasn't going to say anything else. In a few minutes she began to sing, softly, then louder, as if to keep Drew from saying any more.

Alas, my Love! ye do me wrong . . .

"That's it? The new song?"

"It's not new. It's ages old. Everybody knows *Greensleeves* except maybe you, because you were just a year old when Beth died. It was her favorite. Afterwards they all stopped singing it, until Kate came across it in a book the other day and said we should do it again."

Greensleeves was all my joy,
Greensleeves was my delight . . .

Drew walked along beside Betina and listened. He felt strangely unsettled, as if there was something just beyond his grasp, like a word on the tip of his tongue. Then, shaking his head, he ran forward to help Gunther push the cart.

Drew took hold of the handle, and Gunther moved

around to lift the front wheels over the curb. They went along the side of a warehouse, dodging cars turning into a parking lot. They bumped their way across the sidewalk, up and down curbs, past men selling balloons and ice-cream sandwiches and giant pretzels. Cars whisked by on the street, setting up little backwashes of hot summer air.

"You know what, Poppa?" said Drew, swerving to avoid a fire hydrant. "Betina said she isn't going to be here much longer. She's leaving."

Gunther stopped suddenly, so that Drew had to pull back on the cart to keep from running into him. He swung around and stood facing Drew, his mouth opening and closing without a sound. Finally, as if he had decided something, he turned back and started to walk.

A bus pulled up to the curb. "Poppa, I said Betina says she's leaving." Drew pushed his voice up over the noise of the bus. Then, as it moved away, his words were louder than he wanted them to be.

Gunther walked on, without answering.

"Poppa," said Drew, shaking the cart as hard as he could and setting up a jangle of sound.

"It's okay, Drew. I heard you." Gunther started across Pratt Street, tugging the front of the cart, so that Drew had to run, holding on to the handle.

"But don't you care?" he said, once they were on the other side of the street.

"Caring's got nothing to do with it. I don't want her to go—but she's old enough to do what she wants. I won't interfere. I can't," said Gunther. "What people do is up to them. I've always said so."

"But Betina's not so old—and she's not people. She's us—she's your . . ."

"It's still the same. People need to be free to do what they want to do."

Drew wanted to stop, to hold the cart where it was and yell as loud as he could, "It's Betina we're talking about, not people. She says she's going and that she has some place to go. That's why I believe her this time. And I don't want her to go."

Instead, Drew kept quiet, watching as Gunther guided the front end of the cart up Calvert Street to join the others. Together they went past the police barricade and onto Cheapside Street.

"That's why I wanted to leave early," said Gunther, pulling the tarp off the top of the wagon. "So we could set up here tonight, instead of the harbor. I've always liked it here, and I saw in the paper they're closing the street off, to make way for a building."

They took a spot at the far end of the street, lining the campstools in a semicircle, spreading the instruments on a tattered plaid blanket. Kate put the top hat, open end up, at the edge of the blanket, and dropped a crumpled dollar bill inside, then moved along to do the same to an empty banjo case.

Drew took his guitar, settling the strap around his neck, and went to lean against the side of a building. Nicholas did limbering-up exercises, as Kate tuned the mandolin and Betina ran through *Scarborough Fair* on the recorder.

Gunther, carrying his banjo in one hand, strode up and down the street, nodding and smiling and singing, so that before long, he had attracted a following of people, who walked with him, nodding when he did, waiting, as if poised, for the snatches of song he flung back over his shoulder. Drew thought that his father was never so tall as when he was on the streets. Never so alive. And he watched as the rest of them—Nicholas, Kate, and Betina— watched Gunther and at a barely perceptible signal from him came together to take their places. The crowd that had formed behind Gunther moved in close to them as the show began.

3

THEY PLAYED faster, pulling the audience into a circle tight around them, then stopped abruptly, the chords hanging in the air. Kate put her mandolin on the ground, Betina and Drew dropped cross-legged onto the blanket, and Gunther, arms folded, went to stand in back of them.

Nicholas glided forward, speaking to the crowd before it had a chance to stir, to move on.

"I'm Nicholas," he said, bowing with a great sweeping bow from the waist. "And I'm glad to see you here, sirs. Yes indeed, sirs, I am."

"And mesdames, too," he said, stopping in front of a little girl, who giggled and disappeared behind her father's legs.

Nicholas skirted the inner edges of the circle, breaking into a three-ball juggle and keeping up a steady line of patter.

"They tell me it's a block party . . . I brought my friends with me tonight . . . Yes indeed, sirs . . . new friends . . . old friends . . ."

The balls spun higher and higher as Nicholas moved to the side of the circle. "Would you like a little background music?" he asked a woman holding an ice-cream cone.

Nicholas swung around and called to Gunther. "A little music, sir."

Gunther began to clap rhythmically, and Drew watched as his father nodded and beckoned to the crowd around them. Soon they were all clapping, the sound bouncing off the buildings that lined the street.

In the center of the circle, Nicholas sent the balls into a cascade that flowed so quickly it looked like a band of red in the air.

"Enough, sir," he said to Gunther, who held up his hands until the clapping stopped. Nicholas set the balls onto the ground and picked up a yellow club. He tossed it up, spun around, and caught it, working his way sideways, tossing and spinning and catching.

"A one-club pirouette—anybody call for two?"

"Two," someone called.

And there were two clubs rising and falling as Nicholas spun beneath them.

"How about three, sir? Do I hear three?"

"Three." The crowd began to chant. "Three . . . three . . ."

Nicholas stood poised, the clubs held high, his legs bent slightly at the knees. "Three, sirs. Three it is."

He moved as if to raise his arms.

The crowd drew in its breath. And Nicholas spun without tossing the clubs.

The crowd groaned.

"Forgot something, didn't I?" he said, sliding back into the center, feinting and spinning again, without tossing the clubs.

"A-hah—" said Nicholas, stopping still. "I'll bet you think I can't do it. Is that it? Threescore years and ten and can't do a three-club pirouette."

The crowd waited, easing forward.

"Maybe you're right." Nicholas held the clubs, looking at them as if he had never seen them before.

"Yes, sir, you—may—be—" And suddenly the three yellow clubs were spinning in the air, yellow into gold, as Nicholas spun around under them.

"*Wrong*," he said triumphantly, catching the clubs. One —two—three.

The crowd let out its breath and stepped back, but Nicholas immediately pulled them in again as he threw the clubs into the air and repeated his pirouette.

The ground under the blanket was hard and Drew shifted slightly, moving up onto his knees, then down to sit again. He looked at the faces rimming the circle, looking toward him, and for a minute he felt like a zoo animal in a cage. The faces smiled and laughed when Nicholas pretended to miss a catch, then snagged it neatly at the last second. They were long, short, fat, and thin. After a while they began to look like all the faces from all the other times, to blur and run together the way Nicholas's clubs did, forming a streak of color encircling him.

A child from the edge of the crowd moved into the circle, standing close to Nicholas. Drew saw his father step forward and scoop the child up, carrying her out of the circle, talking and laughing with her parents and the people around them, all the while directing their attention to Nicholas, who had started into his finale.

Nicholas finished his act, bowing and moving to the side. The crowd stirred and separated into individuals, stepping forward to drop money into the hat—some of them going on, others taking up new positions to see what would happen next.

Betina nudged him with the side of her foot. "We're on," she said.

Gunther handed the child back to her family and, picking up his guitar, stood beside Kate. Drew followed Betina to his place just in front of them. All around him he heard, beyond the squeak of instruments being tuned, a kind of settling in.

"*Greensleeves*," whispered Gunther, leaning into them. With that the group began to sway, but Drew stood straight and stiff, unsure of the music. He heard them all weaving the strands of melody together. He knew Gunther was staring at him, willing him to play. Betina's voice rose soft and clear:

> *Alas, my Love! ye do me wrong*
> *To cast me off discourteously . . .*

And Drew scrabbled to catch up, trying to play along with the rest of them.

> *And I have loved you so long . . .*

Betina sang.

He was out of time—just beyond the rhythm of the song. The melody had a faster tempo than he remembered.

Drew felt jostled, and slightly rearranged. Then he found himself in a darkly paneled room, sitting on the floor, on straw that prickled his hands. The streets and the crowds and the smell of hot pretzels were gone, but the music was still around him, sliding into the chorus.

> *Greensleeves was all my joy,*
> *Greensleeves was my delight . . .*

He blinked. Something hard and knobby poked against his back, and he looked up at the carved wooden chest behind him. He turned back into the room, toward a woman and a little girl and boy sitting on stools in front of the fireplace. A man and a boy about Drew's age stood beside them. The man, his foot on the rung of one of the stools, was strumming an instrument that, to Drew, looked like Kate's mandolin except that the pegbox was bent back. He plucked at the strings, pulling a sound from them that was both lively and haunting. The boy, his wiry red hair pushing against his flat blue cap, played a recorder. The sound skimmed like birdsong just above the melody.

Drew felt both hot and cold, and his heart thumped inside his chest. Watching the door at the end of the room, he tried to measure the distance as he shifted up onto his knees, ready to run. He took a deep breath, then let it out. I don't know where I am. Or how I got here. Or where the others are. And if I go through that door, I don't even know where I'll be then. Thoughts chased one after another through his head. He edged back into the shadows, cracking his knuckles and wondering what would happen when the people in the room saw him there. His knees hurt from kneeling, and his right foot was asleep. The man, the woman, and the younger children swayed to the beat of the song, looking at the place where Drew was, not seeing him.

Another surge of panic swept over Drew and he looked down to make sure he could see himself. Maybe I'm not real anymore, he thought. Not real at all.

When they came to the end of the second verse, the boy took the recorder away from his mouth and wiped it along his sleeve. He turned and winked at Drew and began to sing the chorus alone in a voice that was high and clear and made the song sound the way Drew knew it should.

Drew sat down and leaned back against the chest, keeping time with the music played by the other boy and feeling that it was all right for him to be there.

When the song ended, the man put his hand on the boy's shoulder and said, "Aye, Symon Ives, that was fine. Fine." Then he laid his instrument on the table. The children stood up, tugging at their mother until she, too, stood and went with them through the door. Drew stayed where he was, his arms folded across his chest, and waited.

He saw the boy named Symon take two apples from a bowl in the center of the table, turn, and beckon to him. Drew hesitated, not sure what to do next. "Come on," said Symon. And after a minute Drew followed him out of the room and up a dark, narrow, winding stairway.

They went on, past landings and doorways. The house seemed to Drew to be much like his own small crowded house. He followed Symon, hearing the rasp of his shoes on the steps, hurrying to keep up. He watched Symon's legs in long, white stockings disappear up under his blue cloak, appear, then disappear again. Looking down, he saw his own faded jeans and Nikes and wondered at the difference.

The room at the top of the stairs was pinched, as though someone had gathered all the upper edges and pulled them together. It reminded Drew of a picture he had seen in a museum once—the same white walls and ceiling, criss-crossed with wooden beams, that had a scrubbed-all-over look. Clothes hung from two hooks to the side of the bed, and the bed itself was low to the floor, covered with what looked like a thick, lumpy quilt. Against one wall there was a chest and, on top of that, a pitcher of water, a towel, and a brick of soap. Drew moved toward the front of the room, stepping close to a dormer window, where the glass was thick and diamond-patterned. Looking through it was like looking through someone else's glasses. The front of the room seemed to tilt forward, leaning out over the street, almost touching the top room of the house across the way. Red-tiled roofs, sprouting chimney pots, rippled out in all directions. He ran his fingers along the lead strips that divided the glass; they were cool to touch.

"You're early—not expected yet. Master Robert said in a while, though I think he meant a while longer. John Oliver hasn't left yet," said Symon from somewhere in back of him. "Catch."

Drew turned just in time to catch the apple as it flew toward the window. "Wow. You'd never make it in the Majors."

"Majors?"

"You know—Major Leagues," said Drew.

"I don't know Major Leagues," said Symon.

"Baseball? The game."

"I don't know baseball. Is it to do with apples? I know archery and bowling, though."

"Not apples. Balls—baseballs. But, anyway, how can

I be early if I didn't know I was coming?" asked Drew, taking a bite of his apple.

"Gadzooks, you don't know anything. First you're early and then you say you didn't know you were to come. How's not to know, with the getting ready and your father binding you over to Master Robert Baker. The indentures had to be signed." Symon flopped down across the bed, which gave out a flat and creaking sound.

"Who's Master Robert Baker?" said Drew, sitting on the floor and leaning against the wall. "And what's he master of, for Pete's sake?"

"Master of me. And John Oliver. And John Adson, who's to come—that's you—the new apprentice, taking John Oliver's place when he goes to serve the Queen. You're to stay here and learn music with Master Robert."

"The man downstairs with the bent-back mandolin?"

"The lute—'for Pete's sake,' " said Symon, shaping the last three words awkwardly, then grinning broadly.

"Okay—the lute."

"Till you're four and twenty," said Symon.

"Four and twenty what?" asked Drew, standing up and looking at Symon, who now sat cross-legged on the bed, his cap off, his hair spiking around his head.

"Years," said Symon. "We're bound over—have to stay —till we're four and twenty years. That's what the indentures say. But i' faith, the master's a good master and Mistress Anne's a fine mistress. Not like some, I hear. And it's a good thing, too, because we come earlier than most, so we can sing before our voices change."

"That's what my father says."

"Then you did know you were to come. If that's what your father says," said Symon, getting off the bed.

"My father did say—but someplace else. I don't think you . . ."

"Where's your cloak—and cap?" asked Symon, moving around to look at the back of Drew's T-shirt. "Flatcaps they call us, and you'd best expect it and pay no mind."

"Call who?" asked Drew.

"Us—the 'prentices." Symon put his cap firmly on his head. "There's six waits, and 'prentices two apiece. That's eighteen of us in all. And—do you know?—the aldermen sent us out into the country once, hired a wagon and four horses to carry us to Hertfordshire, to play for Good Queen Bess."

"For who?" asked Drew. "Did you say Queen?"

"Queen Elizabeth." Symon moved closer, looking at Drew as if he hadn't really seen him before. "You're not—you're not John Adson who's to be the new 'prentice, are you? Not John Adson at all."

"No," said Drew, edging closer to the door. "I tried—I meant—I mean, there you were going on and all . . ."

"Soul and body o' man, if you're not John Adson, who are you then?" Symon said.

"I'm Drew. Andrew Wakeman. And I'm . . ."

"Son of a wait? A 'prentice to a wait?"

"No. I'm not. I told you—"

Drew took a step back as Symon said, "If you're not a 'prentice, what are you then?"

"I'm a street performer. The son of a busker." And somehow, saying it to Symon, Drew liked the way it sounded.

"Is that a vagabond?"

"Well, no. Not exactly."

"Aye, that's good. My father said no son of his was to be a vagabond. He said either learn the weaver's trade along with him, or—if it had to be music—come to London Town to be with my mother's cousin's kin. And now I'm here, with the waits and 'prentices."

Symon began to prance around the room. "There are processions, you know. We go along Cheapside, with devils and other dressed-up creatures to clear the way. With standard-bearers, drums, flutes, hautboy players, and trumpeters. And the London waits all in their blue gowns with red sleeves and caps and silver chains around their necks.

"It's passing fair to see. And Sundays and on holidays there's music at the Royal Exchange. But you'll have to come along and see for yourself someday."

"Well," said Drew, taking another step back. "We play on the streets too, all together—Gunther my father, Kate, Betina, and Nicholas. And me, Drew. And it's fun. Of course, *we* don't have all that stuff you said—devils to clear the way, and flutes and standard-bearers and all—"

"I' faith, there's no reason to be angry, now. I think a vagabond's the finest thing to be—" He punched Drew on the arm. "And music's the finest thing to be a part of."

"But we're not vagabonds. We don't . . . And yes, it is, isn't it? The music, I mean," said Drew, feeling a grin pull across his face.

"And anyway, I'm glad you're here, Drew Wakeman. Because, even though Master Robert's a good master, it's not like at home in Warwickshire, where my three brothers are. And one of them my twin."

Drew heard Symon's voice, which had been loud before, turn suddenly small as he said, "And John Oliver, the other 'prentice here at Master Robert Baker's, is a great grown man, soon to be four and twenty. That's why, when the master said about John Adson coming, I thought it would be a fine thing." Symon's voice started to rise again. "And even if he hasn't yet, and you're not—I'm glad you're here, Drew Wakeman—vagabond. For Pete's sake."

And both boys laughed.

"Well," said Symon. "Now that you're here, there are things to do."

"Wait," said Drew. "That song. The one you sang before, downstairs."

"*Lady Greensleeves?*" asked Symon. "It's fair new and a favorite with Mistress Anne. We learned it for her." He hummed first, then sang:

Alas, my love! ye do me wrong . . .

"It was a favorite of Beth's too. My mother. And Kate said we should do it again and Gunther said okay and we were doing it tonight." Drew was suddenly caught somewhere back in the past—caught somewhere in what he realized now was the future for Symon.

He tried to remember the things that Gunther had said about minstrels and vagabonds, troubadours and waits. His head hurt with trying to remember and from the sound of Symon's voice still going on. "I'll take you to the river and up to Cripplegate . . ."

Drew went to stand by the window, looking at the light, which was starting to pale. He wanted to stay and hear more from the boy Symon; he wanted to leave—to go back, somehow—to where he came from.

"And you'll stay until we're both four and twenty, and then . . ."

Drew began to move, as if by going through the door

and down the narrow stairs he could get away from the throbbing inside his head. He went down to the ground floor, through a room with musical instruments piled all around and the fire already banked for the night, and out the heavy wooden door onto the street. The houses seemed to close in on him and the air smelled sharp and sour. The street was crowded, though the light was beginning to fade.

Drew stood for a moment, unsure of where to go, and then he was caught in the crowd and bumbled along, to the end of one street and onto another. All around him he heard the sound of music, then voices, and clapping hands.

"See. I told you you could do it. The song was fine," Betina said, leaning toward him. And, at a nudge from Gunther, Drew picked up the top hat and moved forward, passing it among the people still crowded around them.

4

THE AIR in the second-floor back bedroom was damp and heavy. Drew sat on his bed and felt it pressing down around him, pushing against his face, matting his hair close to his head, and plastering his T-shirt to his body. He fanned himself with his hands, then flapped the sheet up and down until it looked like some enormous bird stranded there in the dark.

From the other bed came a sudden snorting as Nicholas shifted and burrowed his face in the pillow. Drew stopped short, letting the sheet drop in a final puff of cool air. He didn't want to wake Nicholas. He had watched the old man perform tonight, knew that even the walk over and back was a performance in itself with his bowing, strutting, and calling to passersby. Drew had noticed the slight hesitation in Nicholas's step as he climbed the stairs to bed.

But, even so, tonight Drew wanted room. He wanted to

push back the stale, thick air that seemed to have been caught up in the house for days, smelling of wet towels and dust. He wanted to shove away Nicholas's bed and spread his thoughts out around him.

How can I think, with Nicholas's breath so close I can almost feel it? he wondered, looking again at the sleeping man with one hand flung up on the windowsill. Can't even get close to my own window, for Pete's sake.

Drew eased himself off the bed, taking silent giant steps across the room and out into the hall. He sat down on the bottom step of the stairs leading to Betina's third-floor room, pulled his knees up under his chin, and listened to the night noises. A car went by on the street, and from somewhere there came a distant screech of brakes. He heard Gunther roll over in bed, and Betina cough in the room overhead.

If they're asleep and I'm awake, then I know I'm not dreaming now, thought Drew, as though he were setting out a math problem.

And before that—during the show—when they were all awake, then I must have been awake, too. Unless I was asleep. And dreaming. Only, Gunther would've poked me, and he didn't. And Betina said the song was okay. Anyway, you can't just go to sleep standing up, I don't think. Unless you're a horse or something.

He turned sideways on the step, his back against one wall and his feet pressed against the other. But if I was awake, I couldn't have—wouldn't have— But I did. I know I did.

Drew felt as though he had been holding his breath for a long time and finally let it go. And the thoughts crowded in around him: about Symon, and following him up the steps to the tiny room at the top of that other house; and the song they both had sung. He started to hum the song, then cut it off, not sure what would happen if he kept on going. Not sure he wanted to find out.

Suddenly Drew wanted to jump up, standing in the little hall closed all around with doors, and yell, "Hey, you guys. Listen. Tonight, or sometime—I don't know exactly when—I met this kid and his name was Symon and he lives —is apprenticed to—bound over, he calls it—to this guy Robert Baker. A wait."

He wondered what would happen if he ran into Gunther's room, shook him awake, and said, "Hey, Poppa, I've got to tell you something. There's this kid—Symon Ives— and he lives in London, London Town he calls it, and he told me about processions and singing for the Queen—"

And for a minute he played the scene the rest of the way out. It was as though he could see Gunther drag himself awake, could hear his response. "Yes—well, Drew, I think that's fine. I've always meant for you to be independent. To make friends on your own. Now, tell me about it in the morning, huh?"

He saw himself turning away from his father, saying, "Kate, how about you? I was telling Poppa—was trying to tell Poppa—about this kid Symon and he's got red hair and lives in this house sort of like ours, only higher, and, well—it's not *now*—and he's apprenticed to a wait and I was wondering . . ."

"That's a good idea, Drew," Kate would say. "You should ask your friends over more often. I've told Gunther that. Just let me know when, and I'll go to the store myself. Or somebody will."

At that moment a light was switched on at the top of

the stairs, and Betina stood looking down at him. "What're you doing there?" she asked. "Too hot to sleep? Boy, my room's like an oven. It's a good thing I've got that little fan, only . . ."

"Nicholas was snoring, sort of. And I had to think. Then I got to wondering about—anyway, now that you're here—" Drew twisted around to look up at her. "Something's happened and I think it has to do with the song—*Greensleeves*. You said it was old, but I didn't think you meant *that* old. And now there's this kid Symon and . . ."

"The song was okay. I told you that before," said Betina, brushing damp tendrils of hair away from her forehead. "Now let me by please, I want to go to the bathroom. And don't worry about Nicholas's snoring. After I leave, you can have my room."

Drew stood up to let Betina pass, then he went back to his room and got into bed. In a few minutes he heard her go back upstairs and turn out the light. The house was in darkness.

Thunder rumbled overhead, and Drew was aware that it had been lurking in the distance, forming a background for his thoughts. Now it was all around him, crashing down, rattling the windows and, at times, the brick and plaster of the walls. Wind funneled through the house, swirled up and down the stairwell, circled the landings, slapped at doors, and ruffled bedclothes. The rain pelted down, striking the screen and releasing a wet, dusty smell. It puddled onto the windowsill, turning to a fine spray by the time it reached Drew.

Making his way across the room, Drew leaned over Nicholas and shut the window, looking down at the old man, whose face was pale and covered with raindrops.

Lightning lit the sky, the window, the inside of the room. Drew stood next to the bed and stared at the slackness of Nicholas's face—the pouches of yellow skin underneath the eyes, the soft huffing of the lips.

He's old, Drew said to himself, stumbling over the thought as if it were a footstool that had suddenly been put in his way. As he took the edge of the sheet and wiped the rain from Nicholas's face, hoping he wouldn't wake him, he thought of the old men who sat on steps and watched, waving emptily, as the group trundled its way along the street to work every night. He thought about Nicholas getting old and about the grandparents Betina said they might have, and about Betina herself. What she was going to do. He wondered if Gunther saw what was happening to Nicholas—what was happening to any of them.

Back in his own bed, Drew was careful to keep his eyes on the window, watching lightning streak the sky, then counting until he heard thunder, measuring distances and warding off harm. Nicholas had told him once, when he was small, that if he could see the lightning, it wouldn't hurt him. Drew wasn't sure about this, but he took no chances, staring at the window and listening to the brattle of rain until he fell asleep.

When Drew went downstairs the next morning, Nicholas was already there. His face was pink and clear, and he looked so much like himself that Drew felt as if he had seen a side of Nicholas, the night before, he ought not to have seen.

"What I think I will do today, sir," said Nicholas, climbing up on a red wooden chair, "is clean out this cupboard here. Establish a little order." With that, he began to pull things off the shelves and drop them on the counter—little boxes of bay leaves, oregano, toothpicks, and tins of ginger and allspice.

Drew watched for a minute as jars and boxes and cans were jumbled together. He debated whether to tell Nicholas that Kate had done that very cupboard only the week before, then decided against it, figuring that, in the natural way of things, it could be years before anyone got around to it again. Shrugging, he fixed a bowl of cereal and sat down at the table.

"There's rosemary, 'that's for remembrance,' " said Nicholas, sniffing at a little tin and dropping it onto the pile. "And basil—dill—nutmeg. Here's marjoram, mace, and mustard. Paprika, pepper, and parsley. Cinnamon, cumin, and—" Nicholas tossed three little tin boxes into the air, caught them, and added them to the pile as a fine dusting of spice drifted around him.

"The boys were here, sir. Tom, Dick, and Harry—or whatever," he said, turning from his perch on the chair seat to look down at Drew. "Looking for you. They said they'd be down at the end of the street. For you just to holler, okay?

" 'Matthew, Mark, Luke, and John, the bed be blest that I lie on.' " Nicholas's head disappeared into the now empty cupboard, his voice taking on a funny, rattling tone.

"Yeah, okay," said Drew to Nicholas's back. "And anyway, they're not Matthew, Mark, Luke, John, or Tom, Dick, and Harry either. They're . . ."

But Nicholas wasn't listening.

*   *   *

Drew went out the back door, letting out a loud, full-bodied moosecall. He scaled the fence, hoisted himself up on the roof of the warehouse that boxed in the end of the yard, and repeated the call. He waited until he saw Hank, Jake, and Tom coming up the street and jumped down to meet them. Together they went past the two chalky-yellow railroad cars in the middle of Thames Street, along the chain link fence between the street and the water, thrumming their fingers on the links.

They stopped in front of a freighter that filled all of the space along South Broadway, staring up at the green-and-gray hull that loomed above them, stippled with patterns of sunlight and water.

"Hey," said Jake. "Bet your night last night wasn't anything like ours—the Orioles took them both."

"Wiped the field with the Yankees, man," said Hank.

"First game was six–three. But in the second the Yankees led it all the way to the ninth inning—" said Tom.

"And then—pow—it's the bottom of the ninth and Eddie Murray hits a grand-slam home run and you should've heard 'em—the crowd, I mean. They went wild."

"We told you you should've come," said Jake.

"So—how was it?" asked Hank. "The singing and the music-making?"

"Better than baseball?" asked Jake.

"Knock it off," said Tom.

But Drew was thinking about Symon Ives. All of a sudden he wanted to know more about waits and 'prentices and what it was like to live in London Town. All of a sudden he had to know. Just as he turned to leave, the boys started across the street, heading for the concourse, and Drew was carried along with them.

"So what're we going to do today?" asked Jake.

"I don't know—what's to do?"

"We could go to the harbor and rent paddleboats—"

"If we had any money," said Hank.

"We could go back to the ball park—"

"If we had any money," said Tom.

"We could go to the movies—"

"If we had any money," they all chanted together.

"Hey, you guys," said Drew. "I got to go."

By then, the rest of them were rooting in their pockets, scrounging up nickels and pennies.

"What d'you got?" asked Jake, poking a finger at Drew. "Got any of that singing money, Mr. Greensleeves?"

Drew dug a dime out of his pocket and added it to the pile.

"Nowhere to go with that," said Jake, shaking the coins up and down in his hand.

" 'cept to get some red licorice," said Hank, getting up and leading the way. They went into the market, which was bright and painted white on the inside and seemed to blink at them. They swung up one aisle and down another, past flowers, pasta in bins, and chickens heaped on crushed ice. They swerved around old men with market baskets and women pinching oranges. Finally they lined up across the front of the candy counter, handing over their money for a bunch of licorice sticks.

"Now what?" said Jake as they went outside and stood in the sunlight.

"Stickball," said Hank.

"Yeah," said Tom. They started down Broadway, past the barbershop and the Port Mission. "There's nothing else to do."

"I've got something I have to do," said Drew. But the other boys were a step ahead of him, shoving and jostling as they turned the corner onto Thames Street.

Drew saw the door to the used bookstore standing open. He waited for a moment out front to see if the boys would look over their shoulders, then quickly ducked inside as their voices drifted back to him. "Somebody get the ball and we'll . . ."

Inside the store, the stillness was broken only by a wasp bumbling against the ceiling. As the man at the desk looked up, then down again, a large black cat jumped off his lap and came over to rub against Drew's legs.

Drew ran his fingers along shelves, standing on tiptoe, or stooping down close to the floor. He looked at books on the mantel and on windowsills and piled in laundry baskets on the floor.

"Anything special I can help you with?" the man asked, closing his book on his finger and turning to look at Drew.

"The Queen, sir." Drew thought that he was suddenly sounding like Nicholas.

"There've been lots. Could you narrow it down a bit?"

"Elizabeth—of England, I mean."

"Now?"

"Then. Before. I'm not sure when, exactly."

"Sixteenth century, that'd be. In with history," he said, waving vaguely to the room at the rear of the house.

Drew went up the steps and into the back room and knew at once, from the large settled-down chair, the radio, and a teakettle on a hot plate, that this room was as much living space as store. Bookcases lined the walls, and shorter, stubbier ones formed an island in the middle of the floor. Instead of signs reading FICTION, NONFICTION, and HUMOR, as in the front room, the sections were marked with cards bearing carefully printed messages.

Drew worked his way around the room, past NOT TO GO ANYWHERE, BUT TO GO and HANDMAID TO RELIGION. He paused at HYACINTH AND BISCUITS, trying to decide whether he was in gardening or cookbooks, and was puzzled to see he was in the midst of poetry. Shrugging, he went on, until he came to a sign that said LIFE CAN ONLY BE UNDERSTOOD BACKWARDS; BUT IT MUST BE LIVED FORWARDS. He read it again, moved on, came back and read it one more time, then started to scan the shelves.

"You got it," said the man, who had come to stand in back of him. "But I'm afraid you're out of luck—not much here now. They come and they go. Anything special you wanted to know?"

"That's okay," said Drew, moving toward the door, once again taken with the feeling that he had to hurry on. "I was just looking for someone—something—is all." He went through the front door and out onto the sidewalk and was heading home when he heard the man calling after him. "Hey, you—boy. Try the big library. Uptown. Okay?"

5

WHEN DREW got back to the house, Nicholas was nowhere in sight, and Kate was in the kitchen putting the spices away.

"I did this just last week," she said, shaking a pepper can. "But I guess twice is better than not at all."

"Want me to help?" asked Drew.

"That's okay," Kate said as she earnestly put boxes, one after another, back into the cupboard. "There's something sort of soothing about putting things in order." At this, Drew shook his head and took his peanut-butter-and-jelly sandwich outside.

He found Gunther sitting on a bench, restringing a guitar, the old strings drifting down from a low-hanging tree branch where he had hung them, like strands of a cobweb.

"You look like a spider sitting there," said Drew, taking a bite of his sandwich.

"A-hah," said Gunther, sliding to one end of the bench. "Come into my parlor."

"Ummm—nope. Can't. I'm going to the library. The big one uptown. There's stuff I want to find out about. Stuff I want to know."

"That's nice," said Gunther, pulling the C string taut.

"I went to the used bookstore and the guy there told me I needed to go to the library. Said he didn't have anything. But he looked, though. And asked questions, too." *Ask. Ask. Ask.* Drew said in his head, looking straight at Gunther.

"Ummm, fine." His father took another coil of string from the packet and ran his finger down it.

"Actually, the bookstore has been taken over by a two-headed gorilla," said Drew, shoving the last of his sandwich into his mouth and pacing in a circle in front of Gunther. "He's accompanied by a lion in a sailor suit and seventeen two-toed sloths, and together they plan the overthrow of Baltimore—and maybe the world.

"They have the storeowner in a wooden cage, with only a few crusts of bread.

"Naked."

"Hmmmm," said Gunther. "Fine. Fine."

"Poppa, you're not . . . You haven't been listening."

"Oh—Drew," said Gunther, looking up at him. "Here, hold the end of this string for a minute. You said something, but I . . ."

"I said I was going to the library. And where were we going to sing tonight, 'cause if it's okay, I'll just meet you there. If you can manage the cart and all."

"Oh, that's no problem," said Gunther, leaning back and stretching his legs. "Betina'll help. You run along. Just meet us at Harborplace—across from the *Constellation*. The usual time."

Drew started toward the door, stopped, and turned back to face his father, saying, "Hey, Poppa—if it's just you and Betina bringing the cart along tonight, I guess you wouldn't want to talk to her about—you know—about what she said about leaving and all."

Gunther had his head down and was tuning the guitar, and for a moment Drew thought he wasn't going to answer him. Then his father raised his head, looking, not at him, but somewhere just beyond. "I spoke to her this morning —just to see what she had in mind. And now I can't—I won't—there's nothing I can do."

It was a long way to the library. And hot. The sun beat down and the sidewalk seemed to waver in front of him as Drew made his way through downtown and turned onto Charles Street. He bought a Coke from a man with a pushcart and sat down on a green-and-white bench at a bus stop, holding the icy can against his face before he opened it and began to drink.

He went up the hill, turning at the Basilica and balancing his way along the ledge at the base of the wrought-iron fence, clanking the empty can against the posts, setting up a clackety counterpoint to the sounds of traffic. When the light changed, he ran across the street to the library.

Inside, the building was cool, the stuffy kind of cool that smelled of books and bodies and pencil sharpenings. For a minute Drew stood there in the Central Hall and imagined a giant fan blowing in one end of the library and out the other, churning up great mountains of books, papers, and overdue notices and carrying them along. He went down the back steps and along a corridor of offices to the children's room.

He was glad to see that the goldfish pond was still there, the fish nudging close to the surface and opening and clos-ing their mouths as if they had something important to say. Drew looked down at them, wondering if they could be the same ones which were there when Kate used to bring him and Betina to the library years ago. He remembered drop-ping pennies into the water and making a wish, and Betina reaching her arm in all the way to the shoulder to try and take the money back. The librarian had scolded her, and all the while Kate just sat on the edge of the pond, dangling her fingers and humming under her breath.

He found a book about Queen Elizabeth, but it was tight and dull-looking, one of those books with a plain green cover that never opens all the way out, so he had to keep flattening it with his elbow when he tried to read, and it snapped shut again when he went to turn the page. It was as if he had a crocodile on the table in front of him— a crocodile filled with secrets, and every time Drew tried to reach inside for one, great snapping jaws clamped down on him.

Just then, the door from the hall opened and a woman came in surrounded by little children. Once inside, they spun out in all directions, giggling and tumbling on the floor. They pulled at books and climbed on benches. They stirred the water in the fishpond. The woman grabbed first at one, then at another, and the librarian made fluttering motions with her hands.

Drew felt oversized, the way he had felt once when he went

back to see his first-grade teacher and couldn't fit in the desk. Suddenly he didn't want to be in the children's part of the library with the goldfish and books that snapped like crocodiles. But he wasn't sure he wanted to be in the adult section either, with its silent rooms filled with people piled all around with books. He wasn't sure he wanted to be at the library at all. Even for Symon Ives.

"Anything I can help you with?" asked the librarian, moving a little boy out of the way and coming toward Drew.

"No—that's okay. It's nothing much. I was just—nothing, thanks." He put the book on the table and ran out, back upstairs. He was almost across the main hall, heading for the door, when he saw, out of the corner of his eye, a sign on a desk that read INFORMATION in capital letters. Sliding to a stop, Drew thought for a minute: That means information for me, too. His shoes squeaked against the floor as he turned and went back to the desk.

"I need something about waits, please."

"Weights—well, let me see," the librarian said, taking off his glasses and rubbing the space between his eyes. "Try 'Sports and Recreation'—if you mean lifting weights, that is. Now, weights and measures would be another story. In that case, I'll send you along to 'Business, Science, and Technology.' Then there's boxing—heavyweight and welterweight and . . ."

Drew felt as though he had started something he didn't know how to stop. "No. No," he said, plunging ahead. "Waits—the kind of musician. I know, because all the time Gunther, my father, talks about musicians who play the streets, like we do—all of us—and how, before that, there were troubadours and minstrels and w—"

"You are?" the librarian said, leaning back to see him better, as if focusing a camera. "You do?"

"Yeah—well—"

"A veritable busker, eh?"

"We are—but they weren't, because they were paid by the city, but anyway, I was looking for—a book."

"Oh well, if *that's* the kind of wait you want," the man said in a why-didn't-you-say-so voice. "Upstairs. That'd be in 'Fine Arts and Music,' on the second floor." He waved his hand vaguely at the windows overlooking the main hall as if he expected Drew to just rise up in the air.

Drew went up the stairs at the front of the building, past old men slouching in corners and sitting on the steps. On the second-floor hall he inched his way along as though he were in a hospital, approaching a sickroom. "Fine Arts and Music" sounded formidable. The music part's okay, he thought, looking at the sign over the door. But "Fine Arts" —criminy, I don't even know what they are. And right at that moment Drew wanted to be back at Fells Point, with Jake and Hank and Tom, playing stickball.

He poked his head around the doorframe, then yanked it back. But not in time.

"Come in here. I'm not going to bite you. Come in here, boy."

And Drew went in, sidling up to the desk, looking back over his shoulder and down the aisles, past tables and file cabinets and bookshelves.

"Looking for a way out, eh?" The voice boomed again, echoing from the corners of the room. "A way out—a way out—a way out—"

The woman behind the desk was so small that for a minute Drew looked to see if anyone else had spoken.

"It's me, all right," she said. And when she spoke, Drew saw that her mouth stretched and spread over her face like a red rubber band. "I learned early on that in this life you have to speak up. Say what you mean."

A man working at a table looked up, glowered, and clapped his hands over his ears.

"Now," said the librarian, rising from her chair and leaning forward across the desk and dropping her voice to a gravelly whisper. "What can I do for you? We don't get many of the goldfish set up here, so you must have a very large question. A very important one."

Drew stood up straight. "Yes, ma'am. I was looking for something about waits—they were, . . ."

"I know what waits were," the woman said, scurrying down one of the aisles and back again, plunking a large fat book on the corner of a table and beckoning to Drew. "Now, I'll see what else I can find."

Drew found waits under "W"—and read what he already knew: that waits were musicians employed by the city. They were called waits because they had started out as watchmen, telling the hours at night. By the sixteenth century in England, their only function was to provide musical entertainment. It was as if he could hear Symon's voice telling him this.

"That's not what you were looking for, is it?" The librarian was back, leaning over him.

"No—I mean, I already knew—I guess it was a dumb idea—"

"Of course you knew that," she said, slamming the book and just missing Drew's finger. "Anybody that's heard of waits knows that much." She took the book back to the shelf and nodded for Drew to follow her to the desk.

"There is another book, but it's out. But I tell you what to do." Her voice was booming again. "You leave your name and phone number, and when the book comes in, I'll call you. How about that?" She shoved a pen and paper toward Drew, reading over his shoulder as he wrote.

"A name for a name, Drew Wakeman. I'll tell you my name—if you promise not to laugh. I am Miss Large. Estalina Large."

And Drew heard her laughter all the way down the hall.

Drew's stomach growled so loudly that he was afraid it would drown out the music and the sound of the people clustered there, some standing, some sitting on the stone seats in a semicircle around them.

Drew was hungry. He had gotten to Harborplace just in time to help the rest of the group unload the cart. There hadn't been time for him to get anything to eat before the first set of songs.

He looked out into the audience and they all seemed to be eating something. Drew found himself surrounded by chomping faces, and for a minute it was as if he could hear the sound of tooth against tooth—a crunching, crackling, gnawing sound. It was as though a giant disposal was opening up in front of him, consuming ice-cream cones and pizza, submarine sandwiches, cookies, crab cakes, and strudel.

His stomach whirred again, and Drew shifted from one foot to the other.

"Just one more song and we take a break," said Gunther, stepping slightly forward and measuring the crowd with his eyes. His glance dropped to the upturned hat and the open banjo case, so people instinctively reached into their pockets and opened purses.

They began the introduction of *The Ash-Grove*, Gunther now playing lead guitar. Their feet tapped out the rhythm as Betina and Drew came in together on the first verse:

> *The ash-grove, how graceful,*
> *how plainly 'tis speaking,*
> *The wind through it playing*
> *has language for me . . .*

A motorboat roared into the harbor, drowning out their voices, so that for a moment it was as if Betina and Drew were just mouthing the words. Then Gunther motioned to the rest of the group, drawing them in so that the song grew and swelled and reached to the back edges of the crowd.

> *. . . the ash-grove, the ash-grove*
> *alone is my home.*

"That's all for now, everyone, but we'll be back in a while," said Gunther, stooping to put his guitar in the case and signaling for Kate to wait for the last stragglers before she gathered up the money.

"I'm starving," said Drew. "I'm going to get something to eat."

"I'll hold your guitar if you bring me a Tab," Betina said. "I'll wait over by the bulkhead. And hurry—I have to tell you something."

Drew hurried and slowed himself down at the same time.

He wanted to hear what Betina had to tell him. And he didn't want to hear.

Dashing up the outside stairs of the Light Street Pavilion, he jostled people coming down and wormed his way through the crowd and into the building. Once inside, he ambled along as though he had nothing to do, finally attaching himself to the longest line. He stood hopping from foot to foot, and inching his way up onto the heels of the man in front of him. He wondered again what Betina had to say, and told himself that he didn't care at all.

Drew paid for his food and took the long way out, riding down on the escalator, looking over the heads of the crowd below, and dragging his feet as he went back.

Betina was sitting on the edge of the stone bulkhead, dangling her legs over the side, the instruments piled beside her. "Here's your Tab," said Drew, sitting down next to her, unwrapping his sandwich, and taking a bite.

"What I wanted to tell you . . ."

"I'm starving," said Drew, biting into his sandwich again, as if he could stuff his ears as well as his mouth. "I was at the library and . . ."

"I said before how I was leaving and . . ."

"It's neat here by the *Constellation*," said Drew, waving his sandwich up at the old sailing ship berthed across from where they were sitting. "Y'know it was in the War of 1812—and the Civil War and . . ."

"I don't need a guided tour of the *Constellation*, for crying out loud. I've grown up practically next to it," Betina said. "I want to tell you . . ."

"I'd like to climb it—the rigging, I mean."

"You've always said that."

"I've got it figured out—up the shrouds to the forerigging, and . . ."

"You're doing what the rest of them do," said Betina. "You're not listening to me."

Drew sat for a minute without saying anything. He kicked his heels back against the bulkhead and swallowed hard. "I'm listening, Betina. I don't want to, but I am, okay?"

"I found them."

"Found who?"

"Our grandparents. Beth's parents. I found their name and address—their return address on a letter in Gunther's bureau. It was a letter from just after Beth died . . ."

"You went through Gunther's bureau? Without asking or anything?"

"I wrote to them and mailed it today," Betina went on as if Drew hadn't spoken. "To a little town in North Carolina, and their name is Woodward. Mr. and Mrs. William H. Woodward."

"Maybe they've moved. Maybe they're not there anymore," Drew said.

"They wouldn't have moved." Betina upended her cup, and the ice blew out over the water. "They live in this little town with a main street and porches and neighbors that never change. I'm sure of it. I don't care that Beth left and wandered all around. I want to go there and stay forever."

"They could be dead," said Drew.

"They wouldn't be. I need them there." Betina said it simply, as if her needing them assured that her grandparents would be where she wanted them to be. "I asked if I could come—could stay."

"Did you tell Gunther? Did you tell the others?"

"Just that I wanted to go. There's time enough to say where when I hear from them—from our grandparents," Betina said.

"*If* you hear."

"I'll hear. I'm sure of it. Then'll be time enough to tell Poppa. Not that I think he'll care. You could come, too, Drew. We could go together."

"I don't want to go," said Drew, kicking at the bulkhead again. "And you don't have to go either. You could stay—and change stuff around."

"I don't want to change anything. I can't."

"You could try. We could together."

"You try. Go ahead. Stay and change them, and lots of luck. I want to live like other people. Like people do in magazines, with meals on tables, and days like everybody else's."

Drew wanted to reach out and take hold of Betina's hand the way he had done when he was little and they had gone someplace and he had been afraid of losing her. He wanted to take her hand and hold it as hard as he could. Instead, he found himself inching away from her, sliding along the edge of the concourse and looking down at the water as it blurred before him.

"Come on, kids," called Gunther, coming up in back of them. "Time to get ready. Time for Nicholas to go on. Let's get our places."

Drew stood up, looking at the end of the sandwich he still held in his hand. He hurled it out onto the water and watched the pieces bobble there before he turned and followed Gunther into the crowd.

6

THE ANSWER to Betina's letter came by return mail.

Drew found the envelope on the living-room floor just inside the screen door where the mailman had tossed it along with a bill from the Gas and Electric Company. For a minute he stood looking down at it, reading Betina's name in large curling letters, and was tempted to grind it into the floor with his foot. He knew, by the return address, that it was from his mother's parents. His grandparents.

Drew also knew that the letter had come earlier than his sister thought it would. That she wouldn't be looking for it yet.

I can get rid of it, he said to himself, nudging the envelope with his toe. Tear it up and throw it down the sewer so it'll get all mucked up and go wherever it is that sewers go. And Betina'll never know. It'd be like they never answered her.

He put his foot down on the letter, opened the screen door, slid the envelope over the sill and out onto the sidewalk. Then he picked it up and headed around the corner. Drew stood still for a moment, swaying over the sewer grating. After a while he turned and went back to the house. He put the letter on the floor where he had found it, and ran up the stairs to the third floor, calling for Betina.

Gunther came in just as Betina finished the letter. She swung around, waving the pages at him, stopping to put them back in the envelope before she spoke.

"I've had a letter from my grandparents and I'm going to live with them. I told you I was leaving. I found the address in your drawer and I wrote and—and now—I'm . . ."

Drew heard her voice, which had started out firm, dwindling. But she stood still, without backing away.

Gunther shook his head, pulling at his beard. Finally he said, "Well—yes, Betina, if that's what you want."

No—no, something screamed inside Drew. Don't let her go. She's your daughter. She's my sister. I need her here.

"I went into your room and found the address. It was on a letter they wrote back to you after my mother died. I'm surprised you bothered to tell them she *did* die. There were things you didn't tell them, weren't there?"

Drew felt strangely excited: as if there was going to be a fight where there had never been a fight before. As if they were going to square off, stand up to face one another.

But Gunther turned away, leaning over to finger the open music book on the upright piano.

Drew looked up and saw the rest of them gathered there: Kate at the bottom of the stairs; Nicholas in the kitchen doorway.

"Do you remember what you forgot to tell them?" asked Betina, as Gunther turned back to her. "Do you remember, Poppa? Me. You never bothered to tell them about me. They didn't even know they had a grandchild, and still they want me to come. What do any of you have to say about that?"

The room was heavy with their separate silences. Then Gunther sat down on the piano stool, sighing deeply. "When Beth was alive," he said, looking at Betina, "she was estranged from her parents, for whatever reasons— they were her reasons. So, when you and Drew were born, she chose not to tell them. It was her decision. And after she died, I didn't feel that it was up to me to alter that decision. It had nothing to do with you."

"It had everything to do with me," Betina said.

And me, thought Drew. *And me. And me. And me.*

"You're going to go?" asked Gunther.

"Yes. On Monday. They sent a check and times for the train."

"It's your decision," said Gunther. "As for the money part—there isn't any need. You earn along with the rest of us—the money from the shows. Your share."

"It's almost time," called Nicholas from the kitchen door. "Remember, we're doing our act in the afternoon today. Betina, are you—will you . . ."

"Yes. I'll come as long as I'm here," she said, stuffing the letter into her pocket. "No big deal."

No big deal, thought Drew. Except that Betina's leaving and nobody cares. No big deal, my foot.

"There's just one thing," said Gunther, standing up to face Betina. "Is your brother going with you? Is he going, too?"

Ask me, Drew's thoughts screamed inside of him. Why don't you ask me yourself?

Then Drew saw Betina bite her lip, her face turning pale. He watched as she backed away. "I didn't tell them," she said. "They don't know about Drew."

The crowds at Harborplace were thick, surging around them, threatening to carry them away before they even got set up. The air was filled with the cinnamon smell from the spice company across the street. The wind whipped the edges of the blanket as Kate and Gunther spread it on the ground, putting out the instruments and Nicholas's clubs and balls. Drew stood off to the side, watching the rest of them. He stepped back, trying to disappear into the crowd, but something seemed to hold him, as though he were tethered there. He saw Gunther gathering the people in, his arms outspread. He saw Nicholas doing his exercises, then watched him straighten up, wiping his hands down the sides of his tunic, and stoop to pick up the torches. Betina sat on a corner of the blanket, her arms locked across her chest, her eyes down.

Betina's going.

Betina's going and she can't go.

Betina's going and she can't go, only she's going anyway. Drew's thoughts accumulated like a game of "I pack my grandmother's trunk."

Betina's going and she can't go, only she's going anyway, and Gunther's not doing anything to stop her.

Betina's going and she can't go, only she's going anyway,

and Gunther's not doing anything to stop her, and I don't want to be around to see her go.

"Can't be here," Drew said to himself, breaking into the pattern of his jumbled thoughts. "Won't be here."

He blinked at the thought of Betina's leaving, at the idea of grandparents who, until recently, he hadn't known existed—who still didn't know that he existed. Then he looked up at the sun until its brightness made him turn away. His eyes skimmed along the skyline, across to Federal Hill, coming back to the old frigate *Constellation*.

Just then, he heard the sound of clapping. He saw Nicholas drop onto one knee, blowing kisses. Gunther beckoned for him to join the group.

Drew moved slowly, his feet scuffing against the sidewalk, as he went to stand beside Betina. He heard the squeak of instruments and the flags snapping in the wind. "I'm sorry, Drew," Betina said, without turning her head.

Gunther was poised to play the first note when Drew leaned toward him. "Poppa," he said. "Not *Barbara Allen. Greensleeves.* Can we do *Greensleeves?*"

There was a pause while Gunther seemed to rearrange his thoughts, so that for a moment Drew was sure he was going to play the song he had already planned. Then, as though shifting from one foot to the other, he whispered, "Okay. *Greensleeves.* Because of Drew." And they began to play.

Suddenly it wasn't as bright as it had been. Drew looked up at the sky and was surprised to see houses towering over him. They lined both sides of the street, hooked one onto another, black and white—heavy timbers against what looked like a kind of plaster. The higher the stories rose, the more they bowed out in front, so that the upper windows of the houses on opposite sides of the street loomed close together. Looking up, Drew wondered if two people, one at each window, could lean out and touch hands.

Someone bumped into him, pushing him back against a heavy door with a leather water bucket hanging beside it. A cart trundled by. The narrow street was filled with mud, and a dreadful stench rose up from it. Drew put his hand to his face. He moved back into the street, edging his way past mounds of garbage and he didn't like to think what else. He worked his way up the street, moving through a churning hubbub of people jostling and bouncing into each other. From above his head, he heard someone laugh, and looked up just in time to see the contents of a bucket hurtling down toward him. He jumped sideways, then continued on, scooting past a group of women standing in a circle, hands on their hips, as if at any moment they might break into a dance.

Drew got to the end of the street, turning into a wider, busier one. Both sides of this street were lined with stalls, their canopies rippling in the breeze, the counters cluttered with bird cages, lanterns, and even some kind of traps. He stood still for a minute, feeling as if he had walked into the middle of a movie and couldn't quite catch up with what was going on.

In the center of the street was a fountain clustered about with people washing or filling long, narrow tankards. Farther along, he could see a cross rising above the crowds.

"What d'ye lack, my master? What d'ye lack?" A boy was leaning forward, beckoning over a counter that ran along the front of one of the houses. The boy, in his light blue cloak and flat blue cap, looked familiar to Drew and he darted forward. As soon as he saw his mistake, he stopped, turned, and let himself be bumbled out into the center of the street.

A coach rumbled by, its wheels clattering against the cobbles. Drew pulled back, feeling the ground tremble beneath him.

The air was layered with the sounds of voices, rising and falling around him.

"New brooms, green brooms . . ."

"Buy a mat, gentles, buy a mat . . ."

"Cherry ripe! Cherry ripe! Who'll buy my sweet spring cherries?"

"Sweep, chimney sweep, mistress . . ."

Drew listened to the rhythm of their calls. An old woman pushed a cart piled high with fish in front of him and he caught his breath at the sharp, fishy smell. "Whitings, maids, whitings," she chanted in a singsong. A man stepped away from a bonfire, holding out his arms in a way that reminded Drew of Gunther, and began to sing. Overhead, a sign creaked in the wind.

Just then, someone caught him by the arm, propelling him along, pushing him out of the way of a horse pulling a ramshackle wagon, the driver snoozing on the seat. "You're back."

Drew found himself standing face to face with Symon. "That was a scurvy trick. You were there, then you weren't. I waited and you never . . ."

"I had to go home," Drew began. "To where . . ."

"And then I find you here—in Cheapside," said Symon, gesturing with a long, thin instrument that looked to Drew like an oboe, waving it up and down.

"Cheapside's not here, for Pete's sake. I know Cheapside where I live in . . ."

"If we hadn't been coming through, on our way from practice at Master John Wilson's, me with my shawm." Symon waved the instrument again at Drew, as if he were shaking a fist. "On our way home—by way of Cheapside."

"Symon Ives—we'd best be off. It's dinnertime."

Drew saw the man he remembered as Symon's master, Robert Baker, waiting up ahead with an older boy dressed like Symon. He watched them turn and go on.

"Come along," said Symon, poking at him from behind. "To Milk Street. We'll go home for dinner, and this afternoon, when I have to go with Mistress Anne to London Bridge to shop, you can come. Now that you're here."

Symon moved around in front of Drew, looking him up and down. "But faith—we'd best do something about your clothes. Find you something of mine to wear, so you'll be one of the crowd. So the mistress won't . . ."

"It doesn't make any difference—about the clothes, I mean."

"Why doesn't it make any difference?"

"She can't see me," said Drew. "Not Mistress Anne, or Master Robert Baker, or the two children either." Then, noticing the startled look on Symon's face, he went on quickly. "I know, because the last time I came—the first time I came—when you guys were singing and playing *Greensleeves*, they all looked at me and it was as if they were looking right through me. It was weird—but *you* could see me and, well, it was okay then."

"Zounds," said Symon, pulling Drew to a stop and looking hard at him. "I can—see you."

"I know," said Drew.

"Strange," said Symon, shaking his head. "Come on, then. Let's be off, so we can go to London Bridge."

"London Bridge is falling down, falling down, falling down, London Bridge is falling down—my fair lady," Drew started to sing to himself as he hurried to keep up with Symon.

"It is not," said Symon, dodging around a woman selling cakes. "It is not at all. Why do you sing that song?"

"It's just a song. And a game kids play."

"A jackanapes' song if you ask me. I don't like it." Symon darted out in front, worming his way through the crowd, so that Drew had to run to keep up.

They went along in silence for a few minutes, with Drew always a step behind. Then they turned off the street called Cheapside onto Milk Street, which was smaller and narrower, and stopped in front of one of the houses.

Symon was already pushing his way past the heavy oak door, into the room with instruments cluttered all about that Drew remembered from his other visit. He dropped his shawm onto a table and led Drew into the kitchen. A young boy stood by the fireplace turning meat on a spit, and the room had a warm, crackling smell. Mistress Anne looked up from where she was standing by a table. "Ah, Symon, you're here. Was it a good practice? Take the spit for young William for a bit, will you." She went on without waiting for an answer. "Then we'll have dinner. And mind you, I need you to keep me company on my shopping this afternoon."

Symon turned and made a face at Drew, grinning and waggling his head from side to side. "Aye, mistress. A fine practice," he said.

"Faith, Symon, you look a proper fool, making a face at nothing like that." As the woman moved away from the table, the boys turned to one another, shrugging and laughing. Then Symon motioned Drew through the doorway, whispering, "You can wait out here and I will bring some food. Afterwards."

"Okay," said Drew, realizing for the first time that he was hungry.

"O-kay?" asked Symon, testing the word. "O-kay," he said again. "O-kay. For Pete's sake." He moved back to take the spit from young William.

7

DREW WAITED in a long, narrow garden with a brick wall around it. Flowers tumbled one on top of another, spilling onto the pathway in a tangle of reds, yellows, blues, and whites. The air was sweet, made sweeter by the sun beating down.

He sat on the ground, leaning against the wall, pinching off a piece of honeysuckle. Once, when he and Betina were small, his sister tried to teach him how to suck the honey out, the way the bees did. Remembering this, Drew held the flower up to his mouth and squeezed the end. Then he yanked it away, grinding it between his thumb and fingers, wiping his hand on the ground. He didn't want to think about Betina.

From the open door came the sound of chopping and stirring, the clatter of pewter plates, of a meal being prepared. Gradually, the noises seemed to flatten out, to get farther away. Drew felt somehow distant. The way he felt the time he had tonsillitis and had to stay upstairs in bed listening to the voices of his family down below, who for once happened to be eating all at the same time.

A serving girl came to the door and tossed a cat out into the yard, then went back inside the house. The cat stretched and arched its back, moving toward Drew, but just as the boy reached out to pat it, the animal leaped up onto the wall and sat looking down on the other side. Putting his head back, Drew watched a wasp circle a hollyhock, until, lulled by the droning sound, he began to nod.

"Zounds, I have it. The best that I could get."

Drew opened his eyes in time to see Symon land beside him on the ground in a great churning of dirt and grass and broken flower petals. He righted himself, rubbing at the smudge of grass stain on his white stockings with one hand while he balanced Drew's meal in the other.

"Here's meat," he said, handing a slightly dingy piece of ham to Drew. "And cheese. Bread. And an apple, too. I tried to bring a tankard of ale, but I didn't know how— the rest I just stuffed up under my arm."

Symon sat back on his heels, watching Drew pile bread, meat, and cheese together into a raggedy sandwich. He bit into the apple, then held it up as if surprised to see the hole in it. "Gadzooks—I'm sorry," Symon said, taking another bite. "We'd best hurry, though. Mistress Anne will be ready soon. If you're not hungry, I could help."

"I guess I'm not really. Hungry, I mean," said Drew, holding the sandwich out to him.

Syman looked at it suspiciously for a minute, carefully lifted off the top piece of bread, and ate it. When he had finished that, he reached for the cheese. The ham. The bottom slice of bread. Layer by layer. Then he got up, turning slowly, stretching the way the cat had done a few minutes before. "Are you finished yet?" he asked. "It was just a bit of dinner, after all. And it's time to go. Come *on*."

"Finished? What do you mean, finished? You ate it all. Hey—what's that?" asked Drew, catching hold of the club that swung around Symon's neck.

"Aye—clubs!" said Symon, whipping the strap over his head and brandishing the club as he jumped up onto a wooden bench. "That's what I'm there for. To guard the mistress against ruffians. Any whip-jack or ruffler who tangles with me will get his just deserts." Jumping off the bench, he dropped the club around his neck again and kicked at a clump of grass. "I've never had to use it, though. In fact, I hardly ever get to go. It's usually John Oliver, being bigger and stronger. Me—I get to fetch the water from the conduit. Stuff like that. Oh well," he said, brightening considerably. "Maybe today we'll meet a whole army of rogues and vagabonds. And I'll cudgel them all smartly."

"But how come you have to do that?" asked Drew, getting up and following Symon through the kitchen. "I thought you were an apprentice, here to learn. To study music, like you said."

"Aye—that, too," Symon said. "There's the learning, and the place to stay, the food to eat. In exchange for the stuff I have to do. Don't you—in your—where you—"

"Yep," said Drew, thinking suddenly of the way everybody at home did bits of what had to be done, even if they did all end up doing the same things. "But that's family—I mean, family of a sort. Poppa, Kate, and the rest."

"Well," said Symon, grabbing a pear off the table, "this

is my family of a sort. My father told me I'd best think of it that way. But then, I may be luckier than most."

"But you do miss them—you said so before. Your mother and father, and especially your brothers."

"Aye," said Symon, shrugging. "And if it hadn't been for the music—if I hadn't come because of the music— I'd be off again, back to Warwickshire." Then he went on: "But now there's you. Here. To stay. I knew you'd come back, because you didn't say you wouldn't. The way people have to say things straight out."

"I came because—" began Drew, stopping as Symon turned to face him, hands on his hips.

"Because?"

"Well—yeah—to see you again."

Symon turned and headed into the front room, where sharp sounds of music filled the air.

"And," said Drew all in a rush as he followed, "because my sister Betina's going to leave and nobody's doing anything to stop her. And I don't want to be there to see her go."

In the front room, Master Robert Baker was just putting his lute on the table. He said, "Ah, Symon, mind you take care of the mistress. Walk just ahead and keep your eyes open. I'd send John here, but he needs practice on the new sackbut."

"I will, sir," said Symon. Drew watched as the boy strutted in a circle around the room in time to the music the older apprentice was playing on an instrument like a small, thin trombone. "We'll take good—*I'll* take good care of her," he said as he turned and motioned for Drew to follow him.

* * *

They went across Cheapside, down one narrow, bustling street after another, until they came out between two houses and stood at the top of a flight of steps looking over the water. "What is it?"asked Drew, catching his breath at the blue-and-silvery streak in front of him, which was crowded with swans and boats and barges.

Symon, already leading Mistress Anne down the steep, dirty stairs, looked back over his shoulder. "What is what?" he whispered.

Drew pointed to the water.

"The River Thames, of course," hissed Symon.

"Oh, of course," said Drew under his breath, hurrying to catch up.

"Oars, oars . . ."

"Boat, y'honor, boat!"

"Oars . . ."

The cries rose up around them.

"Eastward ho!" called Symon, raising his hand.

And Drew watched as a small boat swung close to the bottom of the steps. Then, barely hesitating, he followed Symon and Mistress Anne aboard. As he settled into the stern beside Symon, Mistress Anne turned quickly around. "Well, Symon Ives, I think that's too many oatcakes for you. We're listing to one side, wherryman."

And Symon moved toward the other side, trying to balance Drew's weight. He waited until Mistress Anne had looked away, calling and waving to a friend in another wherry. Then he put his hand over his mouth and said, "We'll go to the bridge. We'll take the mistress to the mercer's, where she's sure to take an age looking at cloths and silks, holding them this way and that." Symon swung his arms up as though shaking a bolt of cloth. "Then we'll be off to Southwark. If we were sure there was going to be time, we could go to the playhouse. But i' faith we'd best not. The master'd have my hide if the mistress had to wait."

With that, Symon lunged to one side, reaching overboard and rocking the boat. "Gadzooks—I almost had it. A fish as long as your arm."

"How long, Symon?" asked Mistress Anne, turning back.

"From here to there," said Symon, tracing an arc in the air. "And back again."

Looking over the side, Drew was just in time to see a school of small silver-white fish darting away.

Drew followed Symon and Mistress Anne through the pushing, surging crowd on London Bridge. They went along the covered roadway that led down the center, lined on both sides with houses and shops. Apprentices, in the same light blue that Symon wore, stood in the doorways of their masters' shops, calling, "What d'ye lack, my master. See what ye lack. Pins, points, silk ribbons, or garters."

"Cherries ripe, apples fine," an old woman said, pushing a tray in front of Mistress Anne. Symon jumped back and reached for his club, until his mistress prodded him along.

"Hot fine oatcakes," sang another.

"Small coals . . . small coals . . ."

"Cherries ripe, apples fine . . ."

The noise was deafening, spiraling from one end of the bridge to the other, pressing in against them with the sounds of wheels and voices and the clatter of the wooden pattens on the women's shoes. From down below came the roar of water as it rushed between the arches of the bridge.

After seeing Mistress Anne safely inside the mercer's shop and promising her that he would be back in no time at all, Symon led Drew through the rest of the bridge.

As they came out from under the gate at the south end, Drew and Symon stopped, looking up into the sunlight. "It makes me fair hungry, going through the bridge," said Symon, darting forward and handing a woman a coin in return for two thin flat cakes. "Here—oatcakes. One apiece. And none for you," Symon shouted as he turned, shaking his club at the top of the gate.

Drew turned too, looking where Symon looked. His jaw dropped and his insides tightened as he stared into the leering, gaping faces of heads stuck onto spears at the top of the gate.

"Heads?" he gulped.

"Heads," Symon said. "Traitors—or what once were traitors, only now they've got their just deserts." He tucked his cake up under his chin, stuck his thumbs in his ears, and waggled his fingers at the heads looking down at them.

The boys turned to the right and went along the side of a church, then sat on the ground and leaned back against the damp, cool stone.

"Now," said Symon, biting into his cake. "If you don't like oatcakes, I'll just . . ."

"I do," said Drew, shoving the cake into his mouth, suddenly realizing how hungry he was.

"Did you ask her not to go?" asked Symon, stretching his legs out in front of him.

"Ask who? Not to go where?" said Drew, still thinking about the heads stuck onto spears, and trying not to think of them, because they made his stomach hurt.

"Your sister, Betina. You said that your sister, Betina, was going and nobody was doing anything to stop her. 'Okay'?"

"Yeah, okay. I didn't think you were listening."

"I always listen," Symon said. "But faith, if I had started in about someone named Betina, the mistress would have thought I was a dolt. Did you?"

"Ask her not to go? Yeah—well, I guess. I mean, I asked Gunther to ask her. But he wouldn't, because that's the way he is. The way we all are."

"Gunther?"

"My father. And there are the rest of us. Nicholas—a juggler—"

"I like jugglers," Symon said. "I see them at St. Paul's sometimes . . ."

"Kate, Betina, and me. All together now because we just ended up that way, only Betina says she wants to go and Gunther says okay because people should go the way they want to go."

Symon pulled off his cap and pushed his fingers through his hair. "You have to say it right out—what it is you want people to do." He put his cap on again. "Gadzooks—even if they don't do it, you have to say it out loud. Only, you have to get them to listen first."

"Yeah, but that's the hard part. The listening, I mean. You don't know Gunther, for Pete's sake."

"No matter," said Symon, digging his heels into the dirt and sending up a fine cloud of dust. "You can stay here—

with me at Master Robert Baker's. I'll show you jugglers better than Nicholas. And the Queen's own barge, and together we will . . ."

Drew felt warm from the sun and the oatcake and the sound of what Symon said. Betina and Gunther and the rest of them seemed to be getting farther away.

"Come on," said Symon, jumping up, nudging Drew. "We'd best fetch Mistress Anne."

The boys headed back past the side of the church and the houses clustered around the end of the bridge. As they got just under the gate, they stopped, backed up a few paces, and stood looking at the glowering heads. Then, together, they shook their fists at them.

"You got your just deserts," yelled Drew.

"You did, for Pete's sake," yelled Symon.

8

EVEN BEFORE Drew was all the way awake, he felt
as though he were being swallowed up by bells. They
clanged and they clamored, setting up a noise that bounced
off rooftops and spun from steeple to steeple. The sound
pushed in through windowpanes and walls, up through
the floorboards, twanged against the ropes of the bed,
vibrated through the fillings of his teeth. He opened his
eyes to the pale gray light, then closed them again, wrapping his arm over his head.

"Bells," said Symon as he rolled onto his other side.

"What bells?" said Drew.

"Church bells—all the bells of London," Symon said.

"Why?"

"Faith, it's time to get up. Five o'clock." Symon burrowed deeper into the bed, pulling the last bit of covers
away from Drew.

The bells stopped, one after another, but for a while the after-sound held them and swayed them to its jangled rhythm. Gradually, the quiet inched into the room again, and Drew felt his body unclench as he slid back into sleep.

"You'd best get up, Symon Ives," came a voice from the next room. "The woodbox will need to be filled. And the water to be fetched."

"Aye, John Oliver. You'd best get up yourself," called Symon, his voice muffled by the feather bed.

Then a silence layered down around them, broken only by the sound of a thrush outside the window.

There was a sudden sharp rapping that Drew seemed to pluck out of the air and fit all around with dream pictures. Pattens on cobblestones. Tap. Tap. Tap. Symon's club against Swan Stairs next to the bridge. Tap. Tap. Tap. The traitors' heads impaled on sticks dancing crazily by the Southwark gate. Tap. Tap. Tap.

Tap. Tap. Tap. The noise grew more insistent, resolving itself into the sound of knuckles against a wall. "Aye, boys— John and Symon. The first cock's crowed long since, and you'd best be up."

"It's the mistress," said Symon, rolling out of bed and landing in a heap on the floor. "And it's clean-shirt day, besides." He looked down at his rumpled clothes.

"Remember—it's Sunday—clean-shirt day," Mistress Anne called from the foot of the stairs as she clapped her hands. "Best hurry."

The traitors' heads shuffled out of Drew's consciousness, driven away by the sound of clapping, which still lay lightly on the air. He pulled himself up, sitting in the middle of the bed, opening his eyes carefully, sniffing the armpit of his Orioles T-shirt. "Clean-shirt day?" he said.

"Aye—there's a fine from the master for wearing a foul one. But not for you. Who's to know? Who could tell? Unless they smelled you, of course." Symon, his nose held high, sniffed the air. "Is someone here? I smell something most foul . . ." He flopped back onto the floor, sniffing and laughing.

"Says who?" said Drew, diving across the bed and off into space, landing on top of Symon, so that together they rolled around the floor. "Says who . . . says who . . . says who?"

"Says who?" Symon said. "Okay?"

"Clean shirt," said Drew.

"Mean shirt."

"Clean mean shirt."

"Foul shirt, fine foul shirt," gasped Symon.

"Foul fine shirt. A fine for a foul shirt," Drew choked.

"Says who?" Symon said.

"In faith, Symon Ives. I've heard of talking in your sleep, but talking to yourself awake . . ." said John Oliver from his place in the doorway. "Hurry now. Cast up your bed. And change that shirt," he said, twitching his nose.

The air was thick with waiting when Drew followed Symon into the room at the front of the second floor. Mistress Anne sat on a high oak settle, with young William and Margaret on either side looking as though an invisible spring were about to be sprung that would send them jittering and wiggling across the floor. John Oliver and the serving girl stood in back, leaning against the wall at times, then pulling themselves upright whenever the master looked their way. Master Robert paced back and forth, drumming his fingers against the book he held in his left hand.

"Prayers," hissed Symon to Drew as he went to stand beside the other apprentice.

"Prayers, Symon? We know it's prayers. Didst say prayers?" Master Robert asked, stopping in midpace.

"No, sir—I mean, aye. It was—'God be here' is what I meant to say." Drew saw Symon flatten his cap onto his head and tug at his clean shirt. "God be here, sir."

"Aye, Symon. God be here. And so be the rest of us. Waiting here." He pulled his hand quickly over his mouth and Drew thought he saw him wipe away the shadow of a smile.

When Master Robert began to read from his prayer book, his voice had an almost musical tone, but it soon dipped into singsong. Drew slid down the wall and sat, his head resting against the paneling. The light in the room grew stronger minute by minute, spreading into the corners and setting up reflections in the pewter plates that stood lined along the chest. Dust motes hung suspended in the sunlight, and the air smelled musty and unused. Master Robert's voice rose and fell, broken only by the responses to the prayers. Drew moved along the wall toward the door.

There was a closeness all around him, and he thought of another time, another place. They had all been together— Gunther, Kate, Nicholas, Betina, and himself—at an art festival downtown. After they finished performing, they stayed to watch a puppet show, to drink lemonade, to look at the pictures that circled the inside of a tent. And when a sudden storm came up, Gunther had hurried them all into a cavernous stone church on the other side of the parkway. The church had had the same cool airless feel that the room he was in now did—the same smell of candles, the sound of mumbled amens.

The ceiling had been arched all around and there were statues, crosses, and stained-glass windows. But the best thing by far was the floor, where there were pictures made of bits of stone: birds and beasts and trailing vines that ran from aisle to aisle. Soon Drew and Betina were running with the vines, skipping around corners and past holy-water fonts; slapping their feet down on bunches of grapes and leaf clusters. They sailed down the center aisle, skimming close to the altar. Finally, as they careened around a rack of flickering candles, Gunther had reached out to them, taking each one by the shoulder, shaking, swinging, and slapping at them. Drew remembered with a kind of thrill that the more Gunther shook them, the more he seemed to be seeing them. Right at that moment, Drew wanted that scolding to go on forever.

"What's the matter with you?" Kate was suddenly between them, looking at Gunther. "You know they've never been in a church before. What do you expect? Leave them alone."

Gunther had left them alone. He went to stand outside on the steps in the rain by himself. And Drew, huddled there in the vestibule with the rest of them, knew that the day had lost its luster. That he had lost something he never had.

The feeling of claustrophobia that had been hovering just above him sank in all around him and he jumped up, starting for the door.

Symon's foot shot out, catching him on the shin, tripping him—propelling him into the next room.

As he picked himself up, he heard Master Robert's voice rise out of the humdrum of morning prayers, saying, "Soul and body o' man, Symon Ives. For your conduct this morning, you'll fetch the water *and* fill the woodbox. All before breakfast. And you'd best be off—as soon as prayers are done. Before it's time for church."

Drew went with Symon to the conduit in Cheapside to get water. He helped him with the woodbox, piling Symon's outstretched arms high with bits of wood, and even picking splinters out of his sleeves afterwards. But when Symon left for church, Drew stayed behind in the garden, sitting in the shade of a mulberry tree. He finished the last of his bread, licked the honey off his fingers, and moved out into the sun. Leaning back against the warm bricks, he settled down for a nap.

Suddenly it was as though everything in the garden conspired against him. The wall was hard and the ground was lumpy. But when he shifted his position, the wall became lumpy and the ground hard. A bee hovered above him; birds scolded in the tree overhead; and mulberries plopped around him. He tore at clumps of grass and wiggled his feet inside his shoes and wondered what to do next.

He got up and went inside, through the kitchen and on to what he had come to think of as the music room. There, among the instruments, Drew felt more at home than he did anywhere in the house. He picked up a recorder and held it to his lips, pretending to blow into it, almost hearing the sound of a song spilling out. He moved around the draw table, running his fingers along the sackbut, feeling the curve of the bell. The lute lay on the table, and Drew itched to take it up, to hold it the way he had seen Master Robert hold it. He touched the strings gently, then pulled his hand back, reaching instead for Symon's shawm and blowing into it until a loud, piercing outdoor sound filled the room. Drew dropped the shawm back in its place just as the serving girl came running into the room, flapping her apron at the cat, which lay sleeping on the end of the table.

When Symon came back from church, Drew hung around the corners of the room while he, John, and Master Robert practiced a madrigal. He knew that the waits were playing in a concert tonight at something Symon called the Royal Exchange, and Drew sensed the same excitement as at home when the group was going to perform. He cleared his throat and tried to sing along, but words and music seemed to skitter away from him. He shoved his hands down in his pockets and kicked at a table leg. No one heard him. He felt as though there was something he should do, and remembered how at home it was his job to get the cart and help carry the instruments along.

He slouched out into the garden, but when Symon brought him some meat and bread, he followed him back inside, circling the table and making faces, until Symon laughed so hard he had to be sent away from the table.

"Zounds, you almost got me birched for sure," said Symon as, later in the afternoon, the boys made their way down the steps onto one of the wharves facing onto the Thames.

"There was nobody to talk to," said Drew. "How would you like—I mean, there you were—there you *all* were—talking a mile a minute . . ."

"Aye, we do talk. Sometimes I think that's the best part." Symon sat down, hanging his legs over the side of the wharf, motioning for Drew to sit beside him. He pulled a roll out of his cloak and tore it to bits. "For the swans," he said, handing a pile of bread crumbs to Drew.

After they fed the swans, throwing the crumbs as far out as they could, Symon reached back in his cloak and pulled out two apples and a pile of cakes. "For us," he said, lining them along the blackened wharf.

They finished eating, then threw the apple cores out onto the water, wiping their hands on their clothes. Then, leaning back against a piling, Symon sang the madrigal he had practiced before dinner, stopping at the end of each line for Drew to sing it after him.

"There," said Symon when they had sung the song for the third time all the way through. "You know it too, so now you'll have something to do at the concert tonight. You can sing along with us. Gadzooks," he said, jumping up. "We'd best go. Supper's early, and then to the Exchange. I don't know what time it is."

Drew found a place off to the side, tucking himself in against a pillar with the crowd all around him. He watched the apprentices set out the instruments, and saw the waits, all in their livery of blue gowns with red sleeves and caps, take their places. The air was filled with the familiar sound of instruments being tuned. Drew tapped his foot as the music started. He saw Symon and Master Robert. He blinked his eyes and searched the crowd, hoping for a moment that he might find Gunther there. And Kate, Nicholas, and Betina. Suddenly he wanted them.

*   *   *

"Hey, Drew," whispered Kate, leaning toward him. "That woman—the tiny one over there—she's been watching you all along. Do you know her?"

Drew looked out into the crowd of Harborplace, blinking at the light and mumbling "Fine Arts and Music" under his breath as Estalina Large made her way toward him.

Sidling up close to him as the crowd began to disperse, she said, "That book's not back yet, Drew Wakeman. But it will be, and when it is, I'll be in touch. Just you wait. Just you wait."

And he heard her laugh as she moved away.

9

ALL DAY SUNDAY, Drew watched Betina gather her belongings from around the house. He saw her take those little bits of her life that were also a part of his and stuff them into a canvas duffel bag.

"I don't see why we can't have suitcases like other people do," Betina said, pulling her Norman Rockwell poster off the kitchen wall and leaving an oblong of emptiness next to the refrigerator.

"The kind on wheels, with a strap so you can pull it along. I've seen them in magazines." Betina looked around the room to see what she had missed.

"How come?" said Drew, poking his toe into a hole in the linoleum. "We don't go anyplace, anyway."

"You're right. Just here to there. Back and forth. Glumping everything we own along in a cart, for heaven's sake."

"It's not everything we own. It's just the music part—the instruments. You used to like it. Used to like the way Poppa said we were all part of a long line of minstrels, jongleurs, troubadours, and . . ."

"You sound just like Poppa now. Hey, there's my dolphin mug," Betina said, dumping an assortment of pens and pencils on the counter, wiping the mug on the seat of her shorts. "We got them that time we all went to the amusement park in California. The time you got lost and I found you crying by the bumper cars. Only, you made so much racket some guy at skiball gave us those mugs and made me promise to get you away from there. I took you back to Poppa and the rest . . ."

"And they hadn't missed me yet," Drew said, remembering how he wanted to tell his father about being scared and then found, only how could he tell him he was found when Gunther hadn't even known he was lost. Anyway, Betina was there, still holding on to his hand.

"I'm going on vacations," she said now.

"How come?" said Drew. "I thought you were just going to hunker down in that place in North Carolina."

"Everybody goes on trips. You'll see—I'll send postcards."

"And have a suitcase on a leash you can pull along behind you? Big deal," said Drew, hating the fact that he couldn't turn the things he wanted to say into words.

"Yes," Betina said. "Through train stations and airports. I've never even *been* on a plane." She gave the kitchen one final look and headed into the living room. "Some of this music's mine," she said, riffling through the sheets on the piano. When she picked up the music to *Greensleeves*, Drew held his breath until she put it down again.

"What'll I do if they don't have a piano?"

"Then you'll get your just deserts, I guess," said Drew, without thinking what he was saying.

"Huh? My what? Oh, Drew—look. The ship. Remember the night we played at the craft show, and when we were done, we stood and watched the glassblower. How you went back later on your own and got this for my birthday 'cause you knew how much I love blown glass."

"Yeah," said Drew. "What you really wanted was the kitten, only I thought that was dumb, so I got the ship." He watched her hold the tiny spun-glass ship in her hand. "How're you going to pack that? In a duffel bag, I mean."

Betina put it back on the piano. "I'm not," she said. "I'll leave it here for you."

After his sister went upstairs, Drew looked hard at the ship. By leaving it behind, Betina had made a larger hole than if she had taken it with her.

By noon on Monday, Betina was ready to go. So far, the day had been strangely silent, in a house that was used to silences. All morning long, the rest of them stepped around each other, as if by coming too close they could shatter something that was as fragile as Betina's glass sailing ship.

When Nicholas went outside to practice, he dropped his clubs on the ground and sat, staring at nothing in particular. Inside, Gunther worked on his crossword puzzle, his back curved like a shield. Kate drifted up and down the stairs, carrying brushes and turpentine, tunneling her way through the quiet that filled the house.

Drew watched them all, waiting for someone to say something. Wondering if they all hurt as much as he did.

Betina thumped her duffel bag and guitar case down the

steps and stood rooting through her shoulder bag. Then everyone was there, edging the room, watching her get ready to go.

"How're you going to get to the station?" said Drew, speaking around the knot in his throat. "We don't have a car—and by bus from here . . ."

Then they all began to speak, to one another, and to Betina.

"There isn't any car," Gunther said.

"We should have had one, I always said."

"You can't get to the train by bus from here. Well, I mean, you could, but it would take forever," Kate said.

"You could walk—and I'll carry your stuff," Drew said, moving forward, ready to pick up the duffel bag.

"Too far," said Nicholas.

"Too hot," said Kate.

"We'll take the cart," said Nicholas. "Same as we do every night, sir. And we'll all go along—same as we do every night."

"A taxi," Betina said. "I'll take a taxi by myself. I can get one up on Thames Street."

They crowded out the door, Drew picking up the duffel bag, Kate carrying not only Betina's guitar but one of her own as well. Nicholas led the way toward the corner, tossing a single yellow ball up in the air and catching it with a sharp thwack against his hand, time and time again.

They stood on the corner of Thames Street as cars and trucks rumbled past and a small engine pushed at a freight car in the middle of the street, its wheels screeching against the railroad tracks.

Just like a Pushmi-Pullyu, thought Drew, turning to Betina, already shaping the words to remind her how she used to read Dr. Dolittle stories to him before he could read himself. But Betina had a distant look, as if she were already off somewhere in North Carolina with the grandparents he had never seen.

Gunther hailed a cab and looked surprised when it stopped. Betina reached for the door handle, then pulled her hand back. Nicholas, Kate, and Drew pushed close around them.

"Well—uh, yes . . ." Betina said.

"Well, now . . ." said Gunther.

"We'll write," said Kate.

Don't go, said Drew to himself, the unsaid words pounding inside his head. *Don't go. Don't go. Don't go.*

"It's time to go," Betina said, opening the car door.

The driver put the cab into neutral and sighed.

"Yes, indeed, sir, it's been . . ." Nicholas threw the ball up in the air and caught it.

Don't go, the voices inside Drew's head screamed again. Not like this. By yourself in a cab without . . .

"Okay," said Gunther. "We'll—you—take care."

"No," said Kate, grabbing the cab door out of Betina's hand and pulling it all the way open. "We can't let her go like this. Not alone to the train station. Come on, we're going with her."

Drew looked at Kate and wished that he had said that.

Nicholas flung open the front door, piling the duffel bag onto the seat. Kate was pushing Betina into the cab.

"Only take four," the driver said.

"You next, Drew," Kate said, handing the guitar in to Betina.

"Maybe the duffel should go in the trunk," said Nicholas, reaching in and giving it a tug.

"Four's all that's allowed by law," the driver said, taking off his cap and scratching his head.

"Gunther's next," Kate said. "With the duffel on the floor under everybody's feet. Betina, what time did you say the train . . ."

"*Four,*" bellowed the driver, clamping his hat back on his head. "Four to a cab. What are you—a bunch of flaming nuts or something?"

"Four?" said Gunther.

"Four," said the driver. "One—two—three—"

"Four," said Kate, slamming the back door behind Gunther and climbing into the front seat as the taxi screeched out into traffic.

"I caught the next cab, sir," said Nicholas as he came across the station to Gate 7.

Then they stood there, the five of them, buffered all around with quiet, looking at the ceiling, the floor, the overhead board clicking out arrivals and departures.

"Next to arrive at Gate 7—the Crescent for Washington and points south. Only passengers bearing tickets are allowed on the lower level."

They moved in a body toward the steps, encircling Betina, not saying anything.

Down on the platform, the heat rose up to meet them, pushing out between the railroad ties, bouncing from track to track, richocheting off the overhanging roof. Drew blinked his eyes and squinted to see if the train was coming.

"A little music, sir," said Nicholas, pulling a recorder out of his back pocket, gesturing to Kate to take out her guitar.

"Ah," said Gunther, letting out a deep sigh, as if he

finally knew what to do. "*Ash-Grove*—we'll do *Ash-Grove*." And he walked back and forth along the platform, humming under his breath, until Nicholas with his recorder and Kate with her guitar caught up with him and carried him along.

> *The ash-grove, how graceful,*
> *how plainly 'tis speaking,*
> *The wind through it playing*
> *has language for me . . .*

The music went on, wrapping around them, as the train slid into the station and out again. Taking Betina with it.

10

THE NIGHT after Betina left, they all set off for the harbor as usual. But somehow the way there, through the streets of Fells Point, up President Street, and along Pratt, seemed pocked and unreliable. There were potholes where there had been none before, tripping them and sending them into gutters that dipped crazily against the curbstones. Drew felt the streets turn topsy-turvy beneath him and looked around wildly, only to see passersby going along in a normal, straight up-and-down way. He noticed, however, that Nicholas walked carefully, without nodding or calling out. He saw the tight, drawn look on Kate's face, and the way she steadied herself by holding on to the side of the cart. Gunther walked deliberately out in front.

The wheels of the cart seemed to turn suddenly square, fighting against the street, pulling out in different directions, grinding to a stubborn halt as Drew pushed it up to every curb. He prodded the cart along, bumping it onto sidewalks and down again, while Kate and Nicholas struggled with the other end, and the instruments in their cases twanged as if from far away. He bit his tongue to keep from calling out to Gunther for help.

The humidity hung around them, fuzzing the edges of the houses, muting colors, masking downtown buildings like a scrim. People on steps and corners and thronging to cross the street into Harborplace looked hot and sullen. A street vendor jerked at a heart-shaped silver balloon on a string and then let it go, watching listlessly as it disappeared in the haze. A policeman, his dog at his feet, stood beside a lamppost, swinging a billy club and gazing out over the crowd. Instead of pausing as he usually did to talk about the crowd or the weather, Gunther went on past, stopping only when he reached the center of the concourse. He waited, without turning around, for Drew to catch up.

They unloaded the cart, setting up stools, putting out the instruments and the upturned black top hat, moving within their own ragged patch of quiet in the center of the milling crowd.

Even with Nicholas playing the recorder in Betina's place, the music had a diminished sound. When they all joined in to sing, their voices seemed thin and spindly, letting the noise of boat whistles and car horns slip in around the words of the songs. The people in the circle around them shuffled their feet and talked among themselves.

Drew strummed his guitar as if begging more from it than the instrument was able to give. Kate plucked at her dulcimer, and Gunther broke a string on his guitar, cursing under his breath. Even though he tried to keep up, Drew lost the time of the song, so that through the rest of *Blowin' in the Wind* he sounded like an echo, a measure behind.

The house was more crowded after Betina's going. Something had changed, and it was as though whatever it was stretched from floor to floor, filling corners and cubbyholes. The walls pinched inward, snagging at Gunther and Nicholas as they tried to pass each other on the stairway, sending them off in opposite directions. The roof seemed to tighten overhead, and Kate complained that the rooms were too small, too dim—that she couldn't paint anymore. At table, they jabbed each other with their elbows. They jostled together in doorways and filled the narrow spaces of the yard.

"Well, sir, I don't like to complain," said Nicholas one morning when Gunther had called them together for practice. "But I'm a juggler, not a musician. A showman. A virtuoso. Master of the torch and club. And when I have to play along with the rest of you—speaking as one who is threescore years and ten—well, what I am is too tired for my own act. Worn around the edges. Frazzled. Not sharp enough for the juggling."

"I've got an idea," said Kate, rubbing the belly of the mandolin with the corner of her skirt. "Has anybody seen the young couple who sing on *Constellation* pier? Michael and Mary they're called, and they're just down from New York, where they were part of a larger group that broke up. She plays mandolin and guitar; he plays harmonica—and guitar, too. I watched them the other day and they're good —and the thing is, what I hear anyway, they want to join up with someone. To be part of a group again."

"A-hah," said Nicholas. "Help is on the way."

"Sounds like it's worth a try," said Gunther, tugging at his beard. "Maybe we should listen to them play—and if they're good, well, I guess I could talk to them."

That night, Nicholas sat down after his performance, to rest up for his next act. Drew knew that the music, with just himself, Gunther, and Kate playing, sounded sparse and reedy. And he knew, from the way Gunther frowned and wrinkled his brow, that his father knew it, too.

On the way home, they went past *Constellation* pier, where a young man and woman were singing *Barbara Allen*. But they all just kept on walking, and nobody reminded anyone that they meant to stop and listen.

One Sunday afternoon when they got to the harbor, they found that a magician was in their favorite place.

"See—that's what I mean about the competition on the streets," said Gunther as he led the way farther down the concourse. "All you have to do is mess up once or twice and they're waiting there—ready to take over."

It's all Betina's fault, thought Drew as he spread the instruments on the blanket. The way the group's not as good as it used to be—the way everything's sharp and jangled at home—like we're all the time hitting sour notes. He set out the top hat on the corner of the blanket and settled back to watch Nicholas perform.

"I'm Nicholas," the juggler said, falling into the familiar patter. "And I'm glad to see you here, sirs . . ."

As the routine went on, Drew watched the boats in the harbor, only vaguely aware of the spinning balls, torches, and clubs.

"Ooooooh . . ." the crowd said in one voice, and Drew

looked in time to see one of Nicholas's yellow clubs roll across the ground.

"Your turn," Nicholas called to a woman in the crowd. "Don't let it get away."

The crowd laughed as the woman picked up the club and handed it back to him.

Nicholas started into another pirouette.

He missed again.

It seemed to Drew that this time the "Ooooooh" from the crowd had a longer, flatter sound, that the people in the circle looked down at their feet and started to drift away.

Later on, when they were taking their break, sitting on the grass, Nicholas said, "Maybe I'm getting too old for this. I'm seventy, you know."

And Drew thought how much older seventy sounded than threescore years and ten.

Nicholas went on. "Maybe what I should do now is try to get in touch with my sister in Oregon—if she's still alive."

"Sister?" said Kate.

"Oregon?" said Gunther. "You never said—we never knew you had a sister."

"But how could you not know if she's still . . ." Drew let his question dwindle away. He thought, instead, about Betina, missing her, and wondering if the time would ever come when he and his sister wouldn't know where the other was.

When he looked up, Nicholas was kneading his fingers. Gunther checked his banjo strings, and Kate plucked at blades of grass.

Drew wanted somebody to do something: Kate or Gunther to take Nicholas by the hand, to tell him he was the best juggler in town—or anywhere. For a minute he even wished he were young enough to sit on Nicholas's lap, the way he and Betina used to.

They all sat without saying anything until it was time for the show to begin again.

"The cat has to have her rabies shot," Kate said the next morning at breakfast.

"When are you going to take her?" Gunther asked.

"Why do I have to take her?" said Kate.

"Because," said Gunther.

"Because why?" said Kate.

"It's your cat," said Gunther.

"I could take the cat—" Drew began, then pulled back as if he had touched something hot.

"Since when is it my cat?" said Kate, getting up from the table and putting her tea mug in the sink.

"Since you fed it however many years ago the draggled-looking thing showed up here," said Gunther.

"It sleeps with you," said Kate.

"Only out of self-preservation—you kick," Gunther said.

"Anyway," said Kate, hands on her hips, "I didn't feed it. Betina did. It's Betina's cat."

Drew got up from the table, went through the house and out the front door. He sat on the step, next to Nicholas.

"They're fighting," he said. "About the cat."

"Ah—my kingdom for a cat—only, when Shakespeare said it, it was 'My kingdom for a horse,' " said Nicholas. "But if you ask me, a cat is more apt."

Kate and Gunther came out the door, squeezing past

Drew and Nicholas without saying a word. Kate had the cat wrapped in a towel, and though she and Gunther started down the street together, to Drew it seemed that they were miles apart.

"It stinks around here," Drew said, putting his chin on his knees and staring down at the brick sidewalk. "Ever since Betina left."

"You're right, sir," Nicholas said.

"Everything's all mean and sharp-edged. And it's like Poppa doesn't even care."

"He cares," said Nicholas. "Gunther cares, somewhere inside of him."

"He doesn't let on," said Drew.

"He can't let on. The way a lot of us can't let on."

Drew waited a minute, then said, "The thing I don't understand is, when we go out to sing—the group, I mean —Poppa's so good with the people all around. Gathering them together and . . ."

"Yes. He's safer there," Nicholas said. "He's involved, but not involved, at the same time. Anyway, did you ever think, sir, when you see all those people looking in at us, that maybe in just a little way we're doing what some inside part of each of them wants to be doing. Gunther is good at sharing that with them."

"How come he can share with them and not with us?"

"Because, for some people, sharing with strangers is the easy part. It's his way of reaching out." Nicholas got up and stood looking down at him for a minute before opening the door. "But I guess there's nothing we can do. Some things never change," he said as he went inside.

"Nothing we can do . . . Never change . . ." Nicholas's words hung there, taunting him.

"We should be able to . . . Things should . . ." Drew answered back. He stood up and started down the street, thinking about Estalina Large in the library and what she said about speaking up. "Fat lot she knows," he muttered under his breath.

"Hey, Drew," called Tom, who was leaning against a winch at the end of the street.

Drew went toward him, asking, "Where's everybody?"

"Out—someplace," said Tom. "You doing anything?"

"No—yes—" said Drew. "I mean, there's stuff I'm trying to . . ."

" 'Cause if you're not"—Tom kicked at a clump of grass growing at the side of the street—"I've been meaning to ask you—I got this drum—been fooling around with it. If you're not doing anything, I could show it to you."

"Mmmmm," said Drew, looking out across the river, scarcely hearing Tom's words. "I would—could—but not now. I've got something I have to do." And he turned and went back up the street, trying to look as if there were someplace he had to go.

Drew prowled the waterfront that afternoon, thinking about his father and Kate and Nicholas, himself and Betina. About the things they didn't say and wanted to say. How maybe if Gunther would start—if Gunther *could* start—

He lay on the warehouse roof at the end of the yard, brushing twigs and stones into piles with the side of his hand, and thought that what Gunther needed was someone at the other end. Someone to reach back to his reaching out.

"Like Kate," he said out loud. Then he remembered

their fight about the cat and how she and Gunther walked down the street apart together.

"Or Nicholas." He seemed to hear Nicholas saying again that some things didn't change.

Or me, he thought later as he made himself a sandwich.

Or me, he thought as he pushed the cart toward the harbor.

Or me—or me—or me. The words hammered at him as Gunther and Kate played Vivaldi and the crowd pushed in around them.

Drew listened to the sounds of the guitar and the mandolin coming together to form a melody and knew that he wasn't sure exactly what it was he wanted to say to Gunther, or what he wanted Gunther to say back to him.

While Nicholas juggled, Drew tried to sort it all out—how he had to tell Gunther that even though he hadn't stopped Betina from going, it was all right to care that she was gone. He wanted to hear his father say he cared. He wanted him to make Betina come back.

But what if he doesn't care, Drew thought when he and Kate and Gunther were playing *The Ash-Grove*—and he missed a note.

All the way home, even as he was putting the cart away, Drew thought about Symon Ives, who seemed to be able to say anything. Who said you just had to say things right out loud.

He was still thinking about Symon when he went inside and found his father alone in the living room, idly playing the piano.

"Poppa," said Drew, not thinking anymore. "You do care about her going. About Betina, I mean."

Gunther stood up, looking down at Drew. His jaw tightened, relaxed, tightened again, as if there were words fighting to get out.

Then he turned, raised his hand, and brought it down hard and flat on the spun-glass sailing ship. Spits of glass powdered the top of the piano, and from somewhere deep inside of it came an angry, jagged chord.

11

I TRIED, thought Drew, last thing before he went to sleep at night.

I tried, he thought again the next morning, his hands still clenched into fists from when he had punched his pillow up in the corner of the bed the night before.

"*I tried*," he said out loud to the empty room as he picked his jeans off the floor and put them on. "Tried to talk to Gunther—to make it okay for him."

He rummaged in the top drawer for a clean pair of socks, pulled them on, then shoved his feet into his Nikes without untying them.

"Nicholas was right." He kicked first one dirty sock under the bed, and then the other.

"Estalina Large is a cra-zy lady." He yanked the covers up on the bed.

"And Symon Ives can talk all he wants—to Master

Robert and John Oliver and to his father back in War-wickshire—but it doesn't work for me. It doesn't work here." Drew ran his fingers through his hair without look-ing in the mirror.

"So what? I don't care anyway," he said, pulling the door open with such force that it crashed back against the wall, then swung halfway shut again.

Drew went down the steps and through the living room, trying not to look at the piano. He didn't want to know whether the little pile of crushed glass that had been a sailing ship was still there. He had almost made it, was almost into the kitchen when he stopped, turned, and stared at the bare piano top.

In the kitchen there were dishes in the sink, a grape-fruit rind and a sprinkling of coffee grounds on the drain board, toast crumbs and jelly smears and an empty bread wrapper on the table. Drew held a box of cereal under his chin while he got out milk and a bowl, put them on the table, then poked at the mess in the sink. He tilted cold water out of a pitcher, scraped at dried cornflakes, and stood for a minute holding a soggy tea bag. Making a face, he dropped it all back in the sink and turned away.

It can stay that way for all I care, he thought. I'm not going to be here. Startled, he looked back at the sink as if it had told him something he didn't know he knew, then said the words over to himself. "I'm not going to be here."

Betina was right, he thought, fixing his cereal and sitting at one end of the table.

Right to go. Right about not trying to change stuff. And now I'm going, too—but not to North Carolina and a set of grandparents I don't even know.

"Practice, sir," said Nicholas, coming into the kitchen and dropping a coffee mug into the sink. "Your father's waiting out back—we'll practice there because it's so hot inside."

"Time for practice," said Kate, stopping to pour turpentine into a yellow vase, stuffing her paintbrushes down inside. "Come on, Drew," she said as she wiped her hands on her shirttail and headed for the door.

He followed Nicholas and Kate to the yard, where Gunther waited by the mulberry tree. Drew went through the practice motions, thinking "It's the last time" over and over, fitting the words to the rhythm of the songs. The sky was cloudy, but the heat settled down around them, making Drew's hands sweat and feel slippery on the recorder when Gunther made him play *Scarborough Fair* three times in a row. Until he got the tempo right. Every time he looked at Gunther, his father seemed to be looking the other way.

He listened to Kate sing *Blowin' in the Wind* and watched Nicholas juggle four balls while he bounced a fifth one off his forehead. He felt a gnawing pain somewhere inside of him because of what he was about to do.

Then he thought about Symon, and how he said Drew could stay with him, there in Master Robert Baker's house.

"I want to sing *Greensleeves*," Drew said to Gunther when they got to the harbor that night. "We've got to sing it tonight."

"Later," said Gunther.

And Drew stood back, listening and singing along. He looked at the crowd around them, at the instruments on the blanket, the open guitar case with the money inside, at the frigate *Constellation* just across from them, its rigging stark against the fading summer light.

They were almost at the end of the first set of songs when Drew turned to Gunther and said again, "Poppa, please. Don't forget *Greensleeves.*"

As his father began to play, Drew felt an excitement rising inside of him. He put his guitar down, took his recorder out of his pocket, and joined in the introduction. Then they all began to sing,

> *Alas, my Love! ye do me wrong*
> *To cast me off discourteously . . .*

"I'm back," said Drew out loud to himself as he hurried along Milk Street, hopping over piles of rubbish, jumping back as a cart trundled down the street. He turned at a dark, narrow alleyway between two houses, scaled the wall, and sat perched on top of it, looking into the garden at the back of Master Robert Baker's house. The quiet, in contrast to the clamor of the street in front, settled all around him.

"I'm *back*," he said.

"*I'm* back."

"*I'm back I'm back I'm back*," said Drew, jumping off the wall and walking from bush to tree to flower as if reclaiming something for his own.

"*Look out!*" The voice seemed to come from high and far away. Drew looked up just in time to see Symon's head pull quickly inside the very topmost window as what looked like a red ball came flying toward him. He put out his hands, then pulled them suddenly away as the spinning object hit the ground and the tart, warm smell of apple spilled out.

From inside the house came a clattering of footsteps, and in a minute Symon pushed his way through the door and was standing beside him. "You missed," he said, kicking at the piece of splattered fruit.

"Yeah," said Drew.

"Gadzooks, you'd never make it in the Majors," Symon said, grinning wildly.

"Majors?" said Drew. "I don't know Majors."

"Baseball," said Symon, pulling two apples from inside his cloak and handing one to Drew. "I knew you would come back."

"Yeah—well, I did. And I will if it's okay. Stay, I mean."

"Aye," said Symon. "It's passing sweet. It's okay. Now quick—before Mistress Anne needs water from the conduit or a ha'penny's worth of milk. Come up to the room. You know the way."

And Drew followed Symon up the steps to the room at the top of the house.

"Here," said Symon, pulling a shirt off one of the hooks and moving it to the other. "Here—a hook for you. For your clean shirt. And here—" Symon jumped up on the bed, teetering back and forth as he drew an indentation down the middle with one foot while he tried to keep his balance on the other. "Your half.

"And *here*—" He went from the bed to the chest against the wall, pushing at an assortment of stones, a slingshot, a bird's nest holding several eggs, which to Drew's way of thinking were already sending up a putrid smell, and a small kind of paddle with letters written on it.

"Your part of the chest. And the pitcher and the water and the soap—methinks there's enough there for the two of us. More than enough," Symon said, screwing up his face.

"Now—for your own goods. Where?—what?—didst not bring . . . ?"

"I forgot," said Drew, looking from the empty spot on the chest to Symon's expectant face. "I mean, I didn't forget, I just thought—well—I guess I didn't think."

"No harm done," said Symon, yanking a shirt off his hook and hanging it on the hook next to it. "One for each, and we'll take turns wearing them. A little wear and a little air—who's to know the difference."

Drew rooted in the pockets of his jeans, anxious to find something to put on his side of the ewer filled with water. His fingers closed around four gum balls and he lined them on the chest—red, green, yellow, and blue. In another pocket he stuck his finger on something sharp, then pulled out a large, shiny button with a pin on the back. Sucking his finger, he looked carefully at the letters—yellow against a background of black—that read *"Baltimore Is Best,"* then put the button next to the gum balls.

Symon waited beside him, jiggering from one foot to the other, as if he clearly expected more from a person who had come to stay.

Reaching into his back pocket, Drew came up with a ballpoint pen, a pad of paper, his library card, a clump of rubber bands, and a collection of nails. He lined them all in a row along the chest, adding his recorder as a kind of exclamation point.

"There. I'm done."

"Done," said Symon. "And now you're here, I'll treat you true—and never speak thee false."

"Yeah—well, okay," said Drew, scuffing one shoe against the other. "Whatever you say."

But Symon was moving back and forth in front of the chest, his finger hovering just above Drew's collection of things.

"What's that?" he said, stabbing at the air above the black-and-yellow button. "What does it say?"

Drew picked the button up, balancing it on the palm of his hand, before he handed it to Symon.

"*Baltimore Is Best,*" he said, pointing to the words.

"Who's Baltimore?" Symon said.

"It's not a who, it's a what. A place. A city."

"Like London is a city?"

"Like London is a city," said Drew, moving closer to the window and peering down at the street below. "Sort of."

Symon pinned the button on his cloak and angled himself in front of the window to try to catch his reflection.

"You know something I forgot," said Drew. "I guess you're right. Baltimore is a person, too—or was. There was *Lord* Baltimore—a bunch of them, I think. And he was from here—the first one, anyway."

"Here where?" said Symon, looking quickly around the room as if expecting to find someone.

"Here—England. And he went—or sent someone—I forget which—to settle Maryland. On a grant from King James I."

"King who?"

"King James."

"There wasn't any," said Symon, moving the button from one side of his cloak to the other, and looking at himself in the window again.

"There was—or there's going to be. Oh, never mind," Drew said, feeling suddenly caught in a tangle of time. "What's this?" he asked, picking up the small paddle-shaped thing.

"I' faith—my hornbook. With the letters on it. And the vowels—a-e-i-o-u," he said, pointing. "And the Lord's Prayer. My father sent it with me from home, so I wouldn't forget."

"With the plastic on it to keep it clean?" said Drew.

"What plastic?" asked Symon, crackling the protective sheet. "That's horn. I said hornbook, didn't I? What's *this*?" he asked, picking up the ball-point pen.

"A pen—for writing with."

"Where's the goose quill?" said Symon, turning the pen over and over.

"There isn't any. Here—you work it like this." Drew pushed at the chrome button at the end and picked up the pad of paper, making squiggles on the page. "See."

"Aye—let me," said Symon, taking the pen and fitting his fingers clumsily around it and writing slowly in small, cramped letters: *a-e-i-o-u.*

"Gadzooks," he said, resettling the pen between his fingers and turning to another page. He wrote *a-e-i-o-u* again and again in successively larger letters.

"What's *this*?" he said, putting down the pen and paper, picking up the library card.

"My library card. For getting books, you know. You know?"

"I know booksellers. They have their stalls at St. Paul's,

with their 'prentices out in front. 'What d'ye lack, master? What d'ye lack?' We'll go sometime."

Symon took up the pile of nails and jangled them together in his hand; he snapped the rubber bands and ran his fingers down the side of the recorder. "And these?" He rolled the gum balls around the chest, selecting the yellow one and holding it up. "A baseball? For the Majors?"

Drew choked and spluttered, turning away. Trying not to laugh. "No—no. That's a gum ball."

"For throwing? Zounds, it's small enough."

"For chewing," Drew said, grabbing the red ball off the chest, stuffing it in his mouth, and talking around it. "For chewing—and blowing bubbles with. Go ahead. Just don't swallow it."

He watched while Symon popped the yellow gum ball into his mouth, chomping down on it, the look on his face uncertain.

"Again," said Drew. "You have to keep going, and when it's all soft—" He poked his tongue into his own now-pink gum, sticking it out and waggling it up and down. "Then," he said, pulling back his tongue and working the wad of gum to the inside of his cheek, "we'll blow."

Symon bit down again. And again. Slowly at first, then faster and faster. "Hmmmm," he said as a lopsided smile spread across his face.

"Okay—now watch," said Drew, standing directly in front of the other boy and blowing a large pink bubble. He inhaled it back into his mouth, then blew another one, this time letting the bubble stay while Symon moved from side to side to look at it, and finally reached out carefully to touch it.

"Now you," said Drew, working his gum into a flat piece

behind his teeth. "Like this. You sort of squash it down and get it in position there and . . ."

Symon worked his jaws and his lips, opening his mouth to show Drew.

"Now you blow," said Drew, blowing another perfect bubble.

Symon sputtered and spit and slurped. He reworked the gum against his teeth, made hissing noises, and spit some more. He choked and his eyes watered. He sighed, starting over. He flattened the thick pink wad again, pushed with his tongue, and blew. Slowly, a beautiful, large, pink bubble began to grow. It reached out and upwards and sideways, blocking Symon's face and holding there.

"Aye, Symon Ives, hark 'e well," came a voice from downstairs, followed by the staccato sound of clapping. "Wouldst come and turn the spit?"

The bubble popped, spreading a film of fine pink gum across Symon's face, masking his freckles, sticking to his eyebrows and the edges of his hair. "Gadzooks," he said, taking the gum out of his mouth and peeling at the bits on his face. "The mistress—and it's time to go." He watched as Drew put his gum on one of the bedposts, then carefully stuck his on another. "Come on."

12

THE DAYS stretched out, from the ringing of the church bells in the morning to the lighting of the lanthorns outside the houses at dark. In that time Symon had chores to do, songs to be learned. And Drew followed him as closely as his shadow.

Occasionally, there were days when there was no practice, when the wood had been carried early and the water fetched, when Mistress Anne didn't have to be escorted out to shop, or the spit need to be turned. It was then that Symon and Drew ran off, crisscrossing the city from the Tower to St. Paul's, from Newgate to the river. They crammed these parcels of time with so much that often at night, after they were in bed and John Oliver was snoring in the next room, the mice rustling in the walls and the watchman telling the hours, the scenes of the day would spin themselves out in Drew's head until he fell asleep.

* * *

They went one day to St. Paul's—Paul's, Symon called it—pushing their way through the church, which was crowded with people coming and going—peddlers, scriveners, lawyers, gentlemen, and servants. Outside again, they stopped to eat a Banbury cheese and barley cakes, to watch a juggler.

And Drew thought of Nicholas.

From there they went into the courtyard where the booksellers had their stalls. The mob swarmed around them, and 'prentices called out, "What d'ye lack, sir? Buy a fine new play, sir? See a new book come forth, sir?" Then Drew inched closer to the stalls and read the titles: *Arthur of the Round Table . . . Robin Hood.*

He thought of the library and the goldfish and the stale air smell. And of Estalina Large.

Drew thought about Kate and Betina, too. Sometimes, as he followed Symon down Milk Street or along Cheapside, he was sure that he saw them there, weaving their way through the crowds or stopping to shop at a market stall. He would run up close behind a woman or a girl, and just when he was ready to speak or call out, she would turn with a stranger's face—and Drew would drop back, go to find Symon again.

One night, when they were up in their room at the top of the stairs, Drew stood looking out the window.

"I' faith," said Symon, sitting down on the floor, with his back against the bed, "I've waited—but since you've been here you haven't said a word about Gunther, your father—and Betina, who was going to leave."

"She did," said Drew, without turning around. "And he didn't—do anything to stop her, I mean." Drew turned and sat down on the floor, leaning on the wall. "And then afterwards—like you said—I said right out how he didn't *care* about Betina going and . . ."

"And?" said Symon, bending forward, rolling his recorder back and forth between his hands.

"And he smashed Betina's sailing ship—all made of blown glass. Smashed it flat down with his hand." Drew slammed his own hand down on the floor. "So that's when I left—came here—to stay. The way Betina left. And now I'm here and it's all okay and—" Drew let his words wind down.

They sat in silence for a few minutes, until Symon said, "Gadzooks—I didn't say it was magic. Sometimes you have to say things more than once—with no backing away. And sometimes, saying something doesn't mean anything will change." He opened his mouth as if he had more to say, then instead he took up his recorder and began to play the notes of *Greensleeves*, slowly at first, then quicker.

"See that," he said, holding the recorder across to Drew and pointing to the little marks in the wood on either side of the thumbhole. "That's from practicing so much—here with Master Robert Baker, and at home in Warwickshire." He fit his thumbnail into the nicks. "I'll wager there are none on yours," he said, grinning and reaching back to take Drew's recorder off the bed.

"Says who?" said Drew, making a dive at Symon, grabbing the recorder and rubbing his fingers along it.

"What d'you expect, chump? It's plastic—not wood, like yours. Can't make nicks in plastic—I don't think. Besides, it's new. I wore the last one out—practicing so much."

"Chump—chump—chump," said Symon. "If I am a chump, then you are a jackanapes. A dolt. A . . ."

"Wimp," said Drew.

"I don't know wimp," Symon said, starting to play again. "Come on—we'll race. See who's practiced the most."

And he started to play, the melody of *Greensleeves* coming faster and faster, with Drew playing just a half beat behind. The notes spiraled around the room, chasing one another, at times meeting—then racing off again, with Symon out in front, then Drew, then Symon again.

Their cheeks puffed out with laughter and they choked and coughed and stopped playing, rocking backwards and forwards, holding their stomachs, the recorders rolling across the floor.

"I' faith, Symon Ives—what is that noise?" Master Robert called from the bottom of the steps. Symon jumped up and reached for his recorder as he heard the master coming up the stairs.

"What kind of jackanapes trick was that?" Master Robert seemed to fill the whole doorway. "It was almost an echo," he said, looking at Symon's recorder. "You'd best be off to bed. There's a practice in the morning at Master John Wilson's."

Later that night, after he had been asleep, Drew woke up. He heard the watchman going past on the street below, calling, "Four o'clock and all's well . . ."

Untangling himself from the covers, he went across to the window, pushed it open, and stood looking down.

"Four o'clock and all's well . . . Four o'clock . . ." The voice faded as the man moved farther away.

Drew leaned out the window, crinkling his nose at the fetid smell from the street. He turned his face up, feeling the cool night air, sniffing the faint scent of honeysuckle from the gardens crowded in back of the houses. He watched a cloud waft across the face of the moon and saw the roofs and chimney pots turn dark, then light again as the cloud slid off the other side. Moving away from the window, Drew made his way back across the room. He stubbed his toe against a wooden stool, yelped, and fell into bed. Beside him, Symon shifted and settled into sleep again.

Drew lay still for a minute, then flip-flopped from his stomach to his back to his stomach again. He reached up under the bed and tugged at the bristly rope that crossed from side to side.

And the more he tried to sleep, the more thoughts came to nag at him: about Betina—what it was like in North Carolina, did she like it there. And Nicholas—how he was standing the heat. Were the crowds at the harbor good, and had they found anyone else to join the group? Had Kate started a new painting yet?

And finally—he thought about Gunther.

"You're thinking about your father, aren't you?" said Symon from his side of the bed.

"Yeah," said Drew.

"Aye, I could tell," said Symon. "All that great thumping and tossing about. I can always tell."

"Sorry," said Drew. "I mean, I didn't mean—didn't know . . ."

"No harm done," Symon said.

They were quiet for a moment, listening to the first faint sound of birdsong.

"I' faith," said Symon, folding his arms under his head. "This afternoon—if Master Robert doesn't need me—us. If Mistress Anne doesn't. If the day is fair—then methinks we could go to the playhouse. The way we've meant to do." But Symon said the words lightly, as if he were putting his foot to an uncertain step, testing the weight.

"Ummmm," said Drew, folding his own arms in back of his head.

"Aye," said Symon.

They lay in silence then until the light edged in around the window, the watchman came calling five o'clock, and all the church bells of London began to ring.

When Symon went off to practice with Master Robert, John Oliver, and the other waits and apprentices, Drew stayed behind in the garden, wanting suddenly to be alone. But after a while the garden and the wall around it pinched at him like shoes that were too tight. Drew went over the wall and into Milk Street, up onto Cheapside, along to St. Paul's. He went down to the river, then doubled back to Aldergate. He pushed his way through the crowds and the noise and the muck in the streets. He listened to the cries of the street vendors, and of the 'prentices, the clatter of cart wheels. He saw kites flying overhead, waiting for a chance to swoop down and peck at a mound of refuse. All around him, he felt the excitement and the aliveness of the city. But even as he moved, it was as if he knew what it was he had to do.

Drew went back to the garden to wait for Symon.

* * *

"You're going back," said Symon, climbing up on the wall and sitting beside Drew.

"Yeah."

"Because of your father?"

"Yeah," said Drew, kicking his heels back against the bricks. "Because of Poppa and Kate and Nicholas. Because of Betina off in North Carolina . . ."

"With the grandparents," added Symon, jumping down off the wall, standing with his back to Drew.

"And because," said Drew. "Because of you. Sort of. I mean . . ."

"Gadzooks—because of me? How, because of me?"

"Because of the way we've talked here. About all kinds of stuff. It's the talking I've got to take back. To Poppa. To Kate and the rest."

"Aye. The talking. But talking's not just saying words," said Symon, turning to look up at Drew.

"What do you mean? I don't . . ."

"There's the other part—the listening. The hearing. The way my father listened when I said I wanted music instead of the weaver's trade."

"The way you listened when I told about Gunther and Betina," said Drew.

"And the way Master Robert and Mistress Anne listen to John Oliver and to me. To young William and Margaret. But i' faith—wilt come again?"

Drew slid down off the wall, not answering right away; listening, instead, to the sound of bees and the occasional ping of mulberries as they fell to the ground.

"Wilt? Come again?" repeated Symon.

"I don't know. I . . ."

"You could, you know. Anytime. It doesn't matter that

John Oliver is leaving. That John Adson—the new 'prentice —is finally going to come. You can if you need to. You know how—the way—"

"Yeah," said Drew, but he was thinking ahead—to the wars, the discoveries, and all of history yet to come. That had already come. Things he knew about; things he didn't know about—that might clutter up the way.

"Wait," said Symon, turning and running through the door. "Wait—I'll be back. There's something I have to fetch."

He was gone and back again before Drew had a chance to move. "Here—for you—for playing *Greensleeves* on." Symon pushed his recorder toward Drew.

"But you—what will you—hey, wait—" Drew pulled his own recorder out of his jeans pocket and pushed it at Symon. "Here—for playing *Greensleeves* on."

"Aye," said Symon.

"Aye," said Drew.

"And this, too." Symon handed Drew an oatcake. "In case you get hungry."

"Good," said Drew, reaching for the cake. "I'm hungry now."

"And," said Symon, taking one step toward him and stopping. "Godspeed."

"Godspeed," said Drew, turning away.

Drew held the recorder to his lips and blew into it, but after that it was as though the old wooden instrument took his breath and ran away with it. He was aware of Gunther beside him, strumming his guitar, pulling out the slow, haunting notes of *Greensleeves*. He heard Kate with her mandolin on the other side, keeping time with Gunther.

Drew alone was out of time. The notes pulled away from him, tripping up and down, sounding like the song of throstles in the mulberry tree. Sounding the way Symon had taught him to play the times they had sat together, leaning against the wall in the garden at the back of Master Robert Baker's house.

Drew's song skittered on, vigorous and lively, louder and clearer than the way it usually sounded. It broke the tempo of the other players, so that Gunther turned and glowered down at him, then turned away again. And in that split second before he knew his father would look again, Drew took the recorder out of his mouth and held it down by his side. He poked his tongue around the inside of his mouth, tasting the distant taste of oatcakes, and waited for the song to end.

13

"POPPA," said Drew when the instruments, the top hat, and the folding campstools were packed away in the cart. "If you push in the beginning, I'll catch up as soon as I can. I'm starving—I'm having a Big Mac attack, only with ice cream—and if I don't get something to eat, I'll die."

"Okay," said Gunther, hunching his shoulders toward the cart. "But hurry."

"Yeah, sure," said Drew, sinking backwards into the crowd. He watched until he was certain that Gunther was set upon his course, wasn't going to change his mind and bring the whole group along for ice-cream cones. Then he turned and hurried into the pavilion, past potato skins, crabs, and chicken livers, to the ice-cream stand.

"I'll have a single scoop of Oreo ice cream, please—with Snickers on top," said Drew, digging in his pocket for the money and finally scrounging the last dime out of his back pocket, underneath the recorder. It wasn't so much that he was hungry as that, suddenly, he needed a little time to himself.

He ate the ice cream without tasting it. Then, moving off from the counter, he went by the seafood restaurant and out the door. Hot, humid air clamped down around him as he worked his way along the concourse, past the outdoor cafés, the boats tied along the bulkhead, and the place where just a short while ago they had stood to sing. The crowd seemed to be dawdling, hanging around later than usual, as if loath to go back to where it was even hotter and more humid.

Drew went on without thinking, and finally stopped. He sat on a cement wall in front of the Greek Taverna, with a tree growing up in back of him. He heard the clatter of dishes, the clink of silverware and glasses. Bits of conversation swirled around him. The insistence of a Greek dance filled the air. He heard a baby cry, the voices of children, people calling to other people.

Directly across from him was the frigate *Constellation* and Drew found himself staring at it: the black hull trimmed in cream, the gold eagle and stars, four small square windows all in a row.

Off to the side, on the edge of the brick pier where the ship was moored, was an enormous anchor standing at an angle. Two small boys moved round and round it.

Drew looked back at the stern of the ship: at the gold letters spelling out the name. He traced them with his feet on the inside of his tennis shoes as he said them under his breath: C–O–N–S–T–E–L–L–A–T–I–O–N. The music of the Greek dance throbbed around him.

"What are you doing up there?" a woman shrieked. "Anything to get attention!" And Drew turned to see one of the small boys dangling from the crosspiece of the anchor standing on the pier.

"Anything for attention!" the woman said again as she reached for the child.

"You have to get him to listen first," Symon had said.

"Listen— Anything for attention— Listen—" Drew seemed to see the words written across the stern of the ship.

"Listen—attention—listen—"

Somewhere in back of him, the dance ended and another one began.

Drew stood up and started to move, past the anchor and the black iron stands. As he went down the pier, he measured the outline of the old ship with his eyes, saw the lights strung from bow to stern. When he got to the end, he turned and worked his way back, stopping at the small gray building that housed the ticket office and souvenir shop.

WARNING
No Trespassing
Audible and Silent Alarms

The sign, red with yellow letters, was posted on the stairs going up to the gangplank, and again on the office door.

"WARNING . . ." the sign read.

" . . . alarms . . ."

"You have to get him to listen first," Symon had said.

"Listen—attention—listen—"

* * *

Drew took a standing leap. Without thinking about it, he felt himself hanging by his arms from the roof of the entrance building. Hoisting his body up, he dug with his elbows until he landed in a crouch on the gritty tar-paper surface. He stood up, ran across the roof, squeezed his way around the fence, and leaped onto the gangplank. The metal clanked beneath his feet.

"Hey—lookit—a kid up there . . ." came a voice from below.

So much for audible alarms, thought Drew as he swung from the gangplank onto the deck.

The top of the rail came just even with his nose, and for a minute Drew felt as though he were standing in a hole. He looked back over his shoulder at the Aquarium, with its pointed glass peak on top and the blue scalloped waves made of lights along the side. Across the water, he saw the red neon letters of the Domino Sugar sign scrawled against the dark.

The deck seemed to slope downward as he moved toward the stern. He stopped and stood, holding on to the wheel, looking up into the maze of rigging crisscrossing over his head. Drew felt his stomach lurch, so that he held the wheel tighter before cautiously looking up again.

Letting go of the wheel, Drew made his way over to the mizzenmast. He put his hand up and pushed against the solid feel of it. Then, keeping his fingers on it as long as he could, he moved away in carefully measured steps. Even after he had let go of the mast, he kept his arm stretched out, until he was close against the bulwark of the ship.

Drew began to climb. He went up onto a bitt, then over to the rail, catching hold of one of the shrouds as he stood balancing there. Slowly, he turned himself around so that he stood facing into the lines, carefully sliding his left hand around, feeling the rope sting the palm of his hand. The shrouds were so thick he could hardly get hold of them as he pulled himself up, his feet scrabbling below and finally catching on the lowest ratline. He straightened his legs and felt the line jerk beneath him, swaying sharply back and forth. Drew looked up, then suddenly down as the mast, the lines, and the sky spun around him.

"Hey—look. There he is again—"

"He's going up—somebody do something—"

"Get the cop—there's a cop over there. Somebody . . ."

"Hey, kid—"

The voices from down on the ground faded, grew louder, then faded again like a radio gone haywire. Drew eased his hands along the shrouds. He reached up with his foot and found the next line and brought up his other foot, waiting for the movement to stop. He looked straight ahead, through the squares made by the lines, across to the pavilion on the other side.

He slid his hands up, feeling his arms start to tremble. Another step. Sway. Stop. Wait.

Slide. Step. Sway. Stop.

"Look, officer. Up there—crazy kid . . ."

"Who is it?"

There was the sound of a siren, distant and undefined at first. Then closer. Closer.

"I know that kid," a voice said from somewhere below him.

Drew looked down without meaning to: his knees wobbled and his arms tightened into electric jolts of pain.

Faces stared up at him. Leering. Pulsing. He saw the policeman, his dog at his side, and saw the man's mouth open and close as if in slow motion. Heard the words he said. ". . . know that kid . . . Part of the group that sings here every night . . . One of the street singers . . . Lives over in Fells Point someplace . . . Got to get the father . . ."

The air was suddenly alive with the squawking of call boxes. Policemen moved back and forth, pushing back the crowd, looking up at him.

Drew turned away. He slid his left hand up, letting go with his right hand, flexing his fingers and wrist before he clutched the shroud again. He moved his feet one at a time.

Slide. Step. Sway. Stop.

Slide. Step. Sway. Stop.

He looked quickly and saw that the crowd below had grown. He saw that it now snaked its way down the pier and back against the wall in front of the pavilion, and that over on the other side, people formed in knots. But where was Gunther? Why didn't he come?

Slide. Step. Sway. Stop.

The ratlines got shorter, the shrouds closer together, the higher he climbed.

Slide. Step. Sway. Stop.

Drew let go with his left hand and angled his elbow around the line, leaning his face on his arm. The breeze picked up and he felt the rigging sway. His shirt, which was wet with sweat, turned cold.

"They've gone for his father—sent a patrol car round—"

"Don't want to scare him—make him fall—"

"Got to get him off of there."

*   *   *

Drew pushed higher and higher, until he felt, rather than saw, a platform looming over him. Then he looked up, at the opening onto the platform, at another set of lines cutting across his way. He stood frozen there, sizing up the spaces in between. Do I go through? he thought. Around the side?

"The father's here—" came a voice from far away.

"Father's here . . . Father's here . . . Father's here . . ."

"That your kid? Call him, mister. Get that kid down off of there."

"I'm going up," Gunther said.

"I'm going up," Drew heard him say as he swung around the other set of lines, back onto his own, and dragged himself through the opening. "I'm going up," Drew heard him say as he sat on the mizzentop, leaning back against the mast, waiting for his father.

Gunther poked his head through the opening and pulled himself onto the top. His hair bristled around his head and he peered at Drew as if surprised to see him there.

"What are you doing here? What are—why—"

"Because Symon said . . ."

"What is this—some kind of damn game? Run Sheep Run—Hide and Seek—or Simon Says . . ."

"Symon said—" began Drew.

"Simon Said, then," said Gunther, wiping a beading of sweat off his forehead with the back of his hand. "What do you think you're doing?"

"I'm—I was—"

"There I was, almost home—and this police car comes barreling up behind me with this cop inside—blathering on about some jackass kid who's climbing the rigging—

who's at the top of the *Constellation*. And you know what?" Gunther shook his fist, then lurched and reached for the lines again. "It's my kid—my jackass kid."

"But, Poppa—"

"Should've left you there—should've told that cop, he got himself up—let him get himself down. It's no concern of mine. Only here I am." He rubbed a spot in the middle of his forehead, the way Drew had seen him do when he struggled over a crossword puzzle.

"Everything okay up there?" a voice called from down below.

"Need any help getting him down?"

"*No!*" roared Gunther. "It's all *right*." He lowered his voice and said, "See them down there—all waiting for me to bring you down. Now, what do you have to say for yourself—just answer me that."

Drew was suddenly tired all over. His legs ached and there was a blister on the inside of each thumb. Here he was on the fighting top of the *Constellation* with his father, who was talking more than he had ever heard his father talk before. Now Gunther wanted to know what he had to say—and Drew couldn't think of a single word. He pushed farther back against the mast and felt the recorder in his hip pocket sticking into him. He reached to touch it. Then he took a deep breath.

"Fast—you'd better come up with something fast," said Gunther.

"See—it's like this," said Drew, shifting up onto his knees. "Symon said that first you have to get them to listen—"

"Them who?" said Gunther.

"You," said Drew. "All of them—us."

"I'm listening. So what do you have to say?"

"It's just that we're all together, there at the house and in the group, only nobody talks to anybody else—really talks." Drew sat back on his heels, looking beyond Gunther where the lights faded into darkness. "We don't *say* anything," he went on. "It's like the woman at the library—Estalina Large—says . . . about speaking up. It's like Symon said—how it's the listening that matters too. That and the talking.

"We never talked about Betina's going." Drew pressed his hands down flat on the cool, damp platform. "Even if she did want to go, you didn't, we didn't—any of us—do anything to stop her. We didn't even *try*. But we could now—try to get Betina to come back."

All of a sudden Drew ran out of words, except for those that raced inside his head. *This is what I mean. This is what I'm talking about.*

"She might not—come back, I mean. Even with the trying, she might not," said Gunther gruffly.

And Drew thought of Symon and how he said that saying something didn't always mean anything would change.

"Yeah—well—I guess," he said with a shrug.

"Bring him down—or else we're coming up," called a voice from the crowd.

Finally, when Drew thought that all that was going to be said between them *had* been said, and as the crowd rumbled and grumbled down below, Gunther spoke again. "We have to go—get off of here—but maybe we could—we might—well, talk some more when we get down. Come on now. We'll take different sides."

Drew got himself through the opening and back onto the rigging, waiting there until his father was through on the other side, across from him. And as he waited, he thought, Maybe that's all there is. Maybe that's all there will ever be. Except that I said what I wanted to say—and Gunther did come—and he did say we'd talk some more. Drew took his first step down.

The wind blew and the ship creaked beneath them. Drew saw his father's lips moving, but the words he spoke were caught up and blown away.

"Poppa—I can't hear you. What're—"

Gunther raised his voice, calling, ". . . the night you told me you thought Betina was really going to leave—and I told you caring had nothing to do with it . . ."

Drew's arm ached as he waited for him to go on. Then the wind swung around, hurling Gunther's words full face toward him. "I guess—well—maybe I was wrong about that. Maybe caring has everything to do with it."

Gunther put one foot down and then the other, sliding his hands along the shrouds.

Drew did the same on his side.

"We do care—all of us," Gunther went on, flinging the sentence out like a streamer that whipped around them. "About Betina being gone—and you growing up—about Kate—and about Nicholas getting older."

The closer they got to the deck, the farther apart they were, so that Gunther was almost shouting as he said, "But right now what I care about is getting off this miserable boat."

"Ship. It's a ship," called Drew, smiling at first, then starting to laugh.

"Boat—ship—whatever. I'll beat you to the deck."

They worked their way down, Drew on the portside rigging, Gunther on the starboard. Small white lights outlined the ship, and below them, on the ground, the crowd waited.

"I won," said Drew, reaching down with his left foot and touching the rail, feeling his legs start to buckle.

"It's a tie," said Gunther as he climbed down from the rail on the other side and came to join him, reaching out and cuffing him on the arm. "There's one other thing— do you want to tell me who Simon is?"

"Yeah, well, maybe someday."

14

ON THE SATURDAY before Labor Day, Estalina
Large called from the library and spoke to Drew. Her
voice exploded through the telephone receiver, so that
Drew jumped back. "That book you've wanted—waited
for all summer long—is back. The one about the London
waits—I have it here, if you could just . . ."

And because Drew didn't know how to tell her that he
knew more than any book could ever tell him about waits
and apprentice waits he said into the phone to the librarian,
"Swell—thanks. I'll come today, before the show."

It was one of those cool, clear, end-of-vacation days that
mean fall is coming. Drew went along through downtown
and up Charles Street. He went across Mulberry, splunk-
ing his fingers against the black iron fence of the Basilica,

thinking how the last part of summer seemed to have spun faster and faster, so that the days streaked one into another.

He stopped, balancing himself on the ledge, then went on slowly. He moved his hand from picket to picket, counting off one by one the things that had changed, the things that had stayed the same.

Betina hadn't come back.

She wrote letters from North Carolina, and sometimes called by telephone on Saturdays when the rates were lower. Drew called her too, and spoke to the grandparents he had never met, and when they finished talking, Betina spoke to the rest of them: Kate, Nicholas, and Gunther.

In August, Gunther had gone by himself to North Carolina to visit Betina, to meet the parents of Beth.

When he came back, he had that same closed look he used to have before, and went off to sit on the bench in the back yard. Alone, with his guitar. But this time Drew went with him, followed by the others. After a while Gunther began to talk, telling them about the house where Betina lived—which looked like a picture in a magazine—and how that was important to her. And how next year when she and her grandparents were on vacation they would come through Baltimore to see them all. Drew wondered if Betina had a suitcase on a leash yet: he wrote to ask her.

One day, while Gunther was away, Drew had gone to Tom's house and asked if he could see his drum. After he had seen it, and listened to Tom play, he went home and got his guitar and together they worked out an arrangement of *Barbara Allen*, with Drew playing the melody and Tom keeping up the beat, hesitantly at first, then surer, firmer. Afterwards they went out into the street and played stickball.

Drew came to the end of the iron fence and stood for a minute where it right-angled up Cathedral Street. He remembered how Nicholas had said just the other day that being threescore years and ten was fine indeed. And how, as he said it, he held his hands out steady in front of him. "But let me tell you," Nicholas had said. "When the time comes that I'm really missing balls or dropping clubs a lot —well then, sirs, that's the time I've set aside to learn Italian and read *Great Expectations* and paint the living room." From the way Nicholas said it, Drew thought that maybe that might be all right, too.

He jumped off the ledge and ran across the street, stopping by the library window and looking at a sign that read "Summer Reading" and was piled with books and shells and plastic sand buckets. He climbed up into the space beside the window and thought about the group—how its size and shape had changed since Michael and Mary had joined them. How Gunther spoke just the other day of asking François, the mime, to work with them, to see how it would go.

And then Drew thought about the harbor scene Kate had painted on canvas just for him—because it was his favorite of all her paintings; how Nicholas made a frame for it and hung it in the dining room. But on the wall in her room Kate painted a shell, and after that a map of the summer sky, because, as Gunther said, not everything was going to change.

Drew got down from the window niche and went into the library, which had a deserted, holiday feel. He went up the stairs to the second floor, to "Fine Arts and Music."

"Didn't waste any time, did you, boy?" boomed Estalina Large from behind her desk. "I knew you'd come. Can't be a school project all this great long time—just something you wanted to know?"

"Yeah. Yes, ma'am," said Drew.

"Right this way." The woman came out from behind her desk, carrying a thick blue book as though it were a trophy. "Right here. We'll look at it right here."

She put the book on the table, stabbing at the title with her finger. A *History of English Musicians*.

"Look here, Drew. It's all here. All the things you wanted to know." She riffled pages, calling out topics the way a train conductor calls out towns. "Musicians of the City of London. The Company of Musicians. And here—look at this: the Waits of London."

"Yeah, that's—I mean, swell," said Drew, reaching for the book. But Miss Large was off in a flurry of page-turning. "Here—look. Actual records. Actual names. 1548–1571...1579–1590..."

Drew took the book and held it close against his chest.

"Then the Plague would have come," said the librarian.

"Plague? What Plague? When? Are you sure?"

"Course I'm sure, boy. I know my English history. Used to be down in 'History' before I was in 'Fine Arts and Music.' It makes for a well-rounded person, moving about."

"But the Plague," said Drew.

"Bubonic plague. Off and on. It came and went. Had to do with rats and fleas. Filth. And a great surge of it came through in 1592, killing thousands upon thousands."

Estalina Large's voice followed Drew all the way down the hall. "Bubonic plague. Wiped out thousands . . ." He seemed to hear it as he started down the steps. He got to the landing and stopped, sitting down with his back against the marble wall.

An old man with tufts of grayish yellow hair sticking out around his head and dressed in layer after layer of spotted clothes started up the stairs. He stopped before he got to Drew, turned, and sat with his back to him, rocking and mumbling to himself.

For a long time Drew sat holding the book, looking at the old man's back. Then he opened it, turning the pages, slowly at first, then faster, coming at last to the place he wanted. He skimmed the pages until a name jumped out at him.

"Robert Baker," he read. "A London wait. John Wilson —a London wait."

He read further. ". . . Apprentices to the waits . . . John Oliver . . . Symon Ives . . . John Adson . . ."

Drew held his breath and turned the page. He closed his eyes, opened them, and started to read. "Some of the young apprentices grew up to become not only musicians but composers as well . . . Notable among these was Symon Ives, who in the year 1604 went on to write . . ."

Drew closed the book and hugged it to him. Then he got up and edged his way around the man, who was now sleeping with his head against the wall.

"You know something, mister," he said. "It's okay now. It's all okay."

Downstairs, he left the book on the counter instead of checking it out. He went outside and headed down the hill toward the harbor.

"Now for our final song today," Gunther said to the crowd. "*Greensleeves*, okay?" he whispered to the group.

"Poppa, no. Not—" Drew stopped and caught his breath. "Yes, *Greensleeves*. It's okay now."

Gunther played the introduction and Drew stood still, with his hands down by his side.

They started to sing—the rest of them—Gunther, Kate, Michael, and Mary.

> *Alas, my Love! ye do me wrong*
> *To cast me off discourteously . . .*

The crowd was quiet around them. The flags snapped overhead.

> *And I have loved you so long,*
> *Delighting in your company . . .*

The sun shone and there were sounds of boat whistles from the harbor. Drew ran his fingers down the recorder, feeling the little marks on the thumbhole. He started to play the chorus while the others sang.

> *Greensleeves was all my joy,*
> *Greensleeves was my delight;*
> *Greensleeves was my heart of gold,*
> *And who but my Lady Greensleeves.*

The show was over. The people drifted away.

The group packed the instruments in the cart, along with the blanket, the black top hat, and Nicholas's juggling clubs.

Gradually they wound their way through the crowds at

Harborplace, along Pratt Street and over to President, into the edges of Fells Point.

The streets were less congested here and they spread themselves out. Drew and Gunther walked together, pushing the cart. The wheels jolted against the cobblestones and there was an occasional clang from inside the banjo case.

Drew watched the others up ahead: Nicholas, nodding and bowing; Kate, looking back over her shoulder at them; Michael, with his arm around Mary.

"Poppa," said Drew. "There's stuff I want to tell you now. About the waits and 'prentices and another Cheapside. A Queen called Bess, London Bridge, and the traitors' heads.

"Oh—and Poppa—about this kid named Symon Ives."